THE DAY TITO DIED

DIED

Contemporary Slovenian Short Stories

by

Drago Jančar
Brane Gradišnik
Jani Virk
Lela B. Njatin
Andrej Blatnik

FOREST BOOKS
London and Boston

PUBLISHED BY

FOREST BOOKS

20 Forest View, Chingford, London E4 7AY, UK
PO BOX 312, Lincoln Center, MA 01773, USA

FIRST PUBLISHED 1993

Cover picture: IRWIN,
"Fight Against Gravitation", from "Kapital", 1990

Cover design: Janez Zalaznik

Published with the generous financial support of
Vladimir Bartol Foundation.

CONTENTS

DRAGO JANČAR

Translated by Lili Potpara

Drago Jančar, born 1948 in Maribor. Studied law and worked as journalist, dramaturgist and free-lance writer. 1975 sentenced and jailed because of enemy "propaganda". 1985 in the U.S. with Fulbright Fellowship for artists. From 1986 to 1990 president of Slovenian PEN Centre. Now editor at Slovenian Literary Society in Ljubljana. Novels: 'Galley-Slave' (1978), 'Polar Lights' (1983), 'The Mocking Desire' (1992). Books of short stories: 'The Pale Sinner' (1978), 'Death at Mary-of-the-Snows' (1985), 'The Look of an Angel' (1992). Plays: 'The Great Brilliant Waltz' (1985), 'Daedalus (1988)', 'Stakeout at Godot's' (1989). His novels have been translated and published in German, Russian, Czech, Hungarian, Polish, Dutch. Plays produced in the U.S., Hungary, Austria.

DEATH AT
MARY-OF-THE-SNOWS

I n the great and terrible year of 1918, a young doctor, Aleksei Valislyevich Turbin, almost lost his life simply because he had forgotten to remove an officer's cockade from his fur hat. Mihail Bulgakov depicts the event somewhere in his novel The White Guard. *There exists a force which sometimes tempts us to look over the edge of a precipice, which lures us down into the emptiness,* the writer says. And so his hero Turbin, with a cockade, a lethal sign on his forehead, takes ten steps too many into Vladimirova Street instead of on Alekseyev Hill. At that moment, greyish people in army coats descend towards him from Kreshchatik which is enveloped in distant, frosty mist. The young doctor is struck by the mad idea of playing a peace-loving citizen. But on the face of the soldier standing in front of him there first appears an expression of astonishment, and a moment later of incomprehensible, menacing mirth. *The devil,* he shouts to the other who comes running and pulls the breech, *look, an officer.* Turbin understands nothing, but immediately turns into prey with wolfish instincts. A horrible pursuit begins. The entire street is shouting and encouraging the pursuers to kill the officer. Turbin shoots one of the chasers. But the pursuit does not stop. He is hit by a bullet. Finally he is out of breath and hope. He keeps the last bullet for himself. He wants to shoot himself. *Nothing more could happen... And then he saw her, as if in a miracle, by a black, moss-covered wall.* When there is no more hope, when he wants to put an end to his life, the *Saviour*, as the writer calls the sudden female vision, hides him in her home. It seems that he would die of the wound made by the bullet, but *the pain from his head slithers into her miraculous hands*. The wounded doctor, an officer of the Tsarist Army, is secretly taken to his home, but his health worsens again. The wound is joined by typhoid fever. The doctor knows there is very little hope. *It was absolutely clear to everybody that this meant no hope at all.* Turbin is dying. But fate, which forces him to the edge of death, following its impenetrable logic, saves him for a third time. His sister Jelena lights a candle in front of an icon of the Mother of God and kneels before it. *The flame trembled. A long beam was like a chain elongated right to Jelena's eyes. Then her lost eyes distinctly saw that on the face, lined with golden beads, the lips moved and the eyes became so strange that her heart shrivelled with fear and intoxicating happiness. She let herself fall on the floor and remained motionless.*

During the following days Turbin manages to overcome the crisis. He awakens to life with a waxen face, deep wrinkles around the lips and serious eyes. The young officer of the Tsarist Army was destined to die on the terrible run from his pursuers, he was facing death and he came back to life. Who once escapes death, can never forget it. He or she remains marked with its shadow for life, with a waxen face and sombre eyes. Twenty–seven years later, thousands and thousands of kilometers away, in a sequestered European nook which you cannot find on any serious map, a different life story is completed. In the great and terrible year of 1945, suddenly, following the unpredictable, and for the poor human mind, incomprehensible circumstances, the original situation is repeated. There is a Russian doctor, a former officer of the Tsarist Army, in this case called Vladimir Semyonov, there is an approaching army in grey coats and there is the Mother of God. Vladimir Semyonov is marked by the death that he once escaped. He is trying to hide from somebody, and is grateful to an ancient, miraculous rescue. A few years ago he built a chapel near his home and dedicated it to Her, in "eternal gratitude". With a hollow and insane look he searches for a sign on her face. Is he asking for new mercy, a new salvation on his interminable run? Or, is he only trying to understand divine calculations according to which he had to be saved once in order to find himself in the same hopeless situation so many years later? Possibly, the following true story is imprinted on the life of Vladimir Semyonov for one and only one reason: so that the playful will of fate could, in a different place, a different time and among different people, record it as a different version and a different way out of a desperate situation.

In the spring of 1939, a stranger often comes to the villages by the Mura river. He attracts attention with his peculiar linguistic mixture of Russian, German and Slovene words. Most frequently he stops at the chapel of Mary-of-the-Snows, and once, with few words, he tells the local priest that he is a doctor. He makes inquiries about where to start a practice. The priest suggests a larger town, but the stranger with a serious face on which the priest, neither then nor later, can find a single trace of a smile, answers that he is not interested in towns. He would like to work in the country, and when the priest jokingly remarks: At the back of beyond, hidden from God? he gravely and sharply replies: No place is hidden from God. During the stranger's next visit the priest cannot but observe that he is very interested in the huge portrait of Mary on the altar. With slight masculine embarrassment, quite common in the region when discussing religious matters, the priest tells him that Mary-of-the-Snows received her name because a miracle happened during the construction of a church dedicated to Mary somewhere in Italy. The stranger listens to him carefully, a fact well remembered by the priest. He can no longer remember what year the miracle happened, but it was in August, and it suddenly started to snow. It is just a legend, the priest says, but the other shakes his head solemnly and maintains that a thing like this definitely happened. Then he stays away all summer, but in autumn – some people believe that at the end of September – a car arrives from Maribor, loaded with suitcases and carefully wrapped bundles. A fair-haired Russian doctor, in his forties, of delicate physique, by the name of Vladimir Semyonov, which soon becomes famous far and wide, starts general practice in a merchant's house. Before the year is over the silent doctor is the most well-liked person in the area. Speechlessly, he touches wounds and bandages them.

He inhales the odor of sweaty bodies, the stench of liquor and of sour wine coming from his patients' mouths. Without the irritated restlessness typical of physicians he treats their fevers and fears. Whenever they talk of him they soon run out of topics and words. They still know nothing of the serious man with a dark face. He can speak the language, alright, but in his soft Slovene he rarely speaks more than is absolutely necessary. He does not attend the service, but is often seen at solitary hours before the altar dedicated to Mary-of-the-Snows. During the first few years he frequently receives visitors from the town, among them a tall, beautiful woman. In the night, Russian talk drifts from behind the windows, which sometimes turns into rowing. Then the visits stop, and Vladimir Semyonov goes to town less and less frequently. The following years he is alone more and more. In the years of 1936 or 1937 he buys a large factory building at an auction, and puts various pieces of old furniture into it. He turns the ground floor into a consulting room. With extraordinary care he starts treating diseases of the lungs and respiratory system. In the night a light burns in his windows, he is often seen leaning on his balcony at dawn, silently watching the carriages stopping in his yard. Peasants with numb fingers arrange the blankets on their knees and wrap the sick into woollen plaids. The sick, with childish confidence, place their aches and pains into the hands of this curious man. Perhaps Vladimir Semyonov sees in their looks a mixture of humbleness and dark *muzhik* cunning, perhaps he notices their curiosity as they enter the house. But to all appearances these people do not interest him. He meticulously deals with their problems, but not with them. He is interested in something else. He is interested in the news carried by newspapers, and more and more frequently a wireless screeches in his house. But before the rapidly approaching events take place, he does something which is soon known far and near. In the winter of 1938 he saves the only son of a vineyard worker's widow from certain death. In these days and locality, pneumonia is a disease which rather certainly sends people to kingdom come. Especially pneumonia in a vineyard worker's home. That winter, Vladimir Semyonov for many night keeps vigil over the hallucinating boy. He sits by his bed, in a damp and cold cottage lined with clay, between dishes and cloths, together with the whimpering old woman. The recovered boy tries to kiss his hand, he can give nothing else as a token of gratitude, he presses his forehead, still shining with cold beads of sweat, into the physician's palms. The doctor pushes him away. He does not want thanks. The boy should thank her, Mary-of-the-Snows, it was she who restored his health. And then he should thank his mother, who sat awake by his bed praying for him. These words bestow a saintly glory upon him. The village devotees spread the news around, and the story persists for decades after the events that follow.

And these events are approaching rapidly and inevitably. The same year the visits from the town are renewed. There are rumours that he is visited by Duchess Obolenskaya, the widow of Colonel Boris Aleksandrovich, the commander of the unit in Tsarskoe Selo. A number of times Vladimir Semyonov is called on by a bizarre human creature in a long robe, with a dishevelled beard and long, greasy hair. He is called Fedyatin. The doctor's maid has it that the two stay awake all night, and that in the morning the room is filled with cigarette ends and empty bottles. Russian emigrants' visits from Maribor damage the doctor's reputation a little, but he is obviously not concerned about it. However, the visits again suddenly cease. It is unclear why the strange people stopped coming to that isolated place by the Mura. It is unclear what the night-long talks were about. What is clear is that Vladimir Semyonov is suddenly alone again. Perhaps even more alone than ever before. And it seems that he wants it this way. He wants to be alone. People gossip that he is afraid of something, that he has somebody or something after him, which takes away his sleep. The supposition gains ground when, in the spring of 1938, people notice that a chapel is being erected near the doctor's house. The chapel is dedicated to Her, the Saviour, in "eternal gratitude". Saviour from whom or what? It is becoming more and more obvious that Vladimir Semyonov did not choose to live in this area for the fresh air. He chose this nook to hide. However, soon after the chapel is completed, interest in the Russian doctor recedes. On 25th March, Hitler annexes Austria to the Reich, and German uniforms appear on the other side of the

Mura. Even these isolated villages are flooded by news and expectations. In April 1941, the Russian doctor constantly stands on his balcony, smoking cigarette after cigarette and watching the soldiers who are walking to and fro in his yard. A few days later the army retreats, German troops come across the river, bringing German Socialism. Many people, especially the poor, greet them with pleasure. On an October day, the doctor's house is searched and the radio taken away. The radio is returned when he takes two German policemen into the house. When they have a few drinks too many in the village inn, they question him about Russia and Bolsheviks. Vladimir Semyonov does not answer. From then on he locks himself in his room when he hears their nocturnal conversations. The policemen are often changed; in 1944, the last two are called to the front against the Russians. In the summer of 1944, a patient tells Vladimir Semyonov that the Red Army is already in Hungary. Upon hearing the news the doctor turns pale and quickly walks through the door. The winter is long, there is more and more illness, Semyonov lives on black market meat which the patients bring instead of payment. He hardly speaks to anybody. He often goes to Mary–of–the–Snows, he is seen walking up there through the snow–covered fields. A candle is always burning in front of the chapel. One morning his maid finds him drunk, unshaven and with bloodshot eyes. He is sitting in an armchair with the wireless on.

And thus commences the great and terrible spring of 1945. The news that the Russians are in Austria passes from mouth to mouth. The Red Army is approaching the Mura, the old Yugoslav – Austrian border. Huge crowds of Bolsheviks are approaching through the Hungarian plains. Roaring can be heard from the distance. The house of Vladimir Semyonov is cold and neglected. He returns from his long walks through the fields with muddy boots and goes to bed in them. He speaks to no one. Now, a candle burns in his room, too, before an icon of the Mother of God, before her pale face, lined with golden beads. At night, Semyonov's motionless shadow stands on the balcony. Alone, he stands there, listening to the roaring of guns, or perhaps to the stamping of thousands of soldiers in grey coats. In May, hordes of disbanded soldiers wander around the village. Languages and uniforms mingle. An officer shoots a soldier by the road, theft or desertion. The corpse stirs a few times, and rolls into the ditch. The end, it is again the end, and again they are coming.

On 16th May, a village boy in a German uniform, bare-headed and armless, comes running over the bridge. The Red Army is only a few kilometers from the Mura, by the evening, the first Russian regiments will reach the village. At noon, Vladimir Semyonov orders his maid to scrub the mud from the floor, clean the windows, wipe away the cobwebs and dust. Then he goes to the neighbours' and commissions mowers. For a while he watches them cutting the grass in the meadow behind the house with wide strokes, leaving light-green traces. The boys often put the scythes down. They speak of the Russians who are about to cross the river tonight, they look down the road. Everybody is excited, nobody feels like working. The doctor calmly encourages them to finish the work. In the evening he comes out of the house, bringing wine for the tired mowers. He is clean-shaven, composed, wearing a bright suit. Suddenly he walks away, leaving them without the promised wages. Around eleven in the evening, the priest at Mary-of-the-Snows is woken by a knock on the door. When he opens it, there is Vladimir Semyonov, with a pale face and dead serious eyes. He asks for permission to enter the church.

So Vladimir Semyonov is standing before the merciful face of Mary-of-the-Snows, caressed by the flickering flames of the candle and the dark shadows between them. He is standing before the large and gentle figure which, in the cold of the church, silently, with little Jesus in the arms, looks somewhere past him into the darkness behind. This night, shadows dance over the tender features and the pink glow of her face. Semyonov does not kneel, he does not pray for mercy; Semyonov no longer believes that anything could stop the great and terrible army which has come after him, hundreds of thousands of soldiers, and the roaring accompanying them. He is looking into his past life, and asking her solely to help him comprehend this horrible misunderstanding. Images of the mad pursuit flash before his eyes. Images alone, not a single rational thought, there is no answer.

13

Perhaps he, like Turbin, with an officer's cockade – the lethal sign on his forehead – ran before the pursuers, their screams and shots. What dreadful act, or what flight began all this in that remote year of 1918, that he was forced to run incessantly from town to town to finally settle here, where he erected a chapel to Her in "eternal gratitude" and kept coming to gaze into her merciful eyes? Which ice–cold river did he swim, in which damp cellar did he shiver while footsteps echoed outside, under which tree was he freezing, covered with snow, from which bloody ditch did he climb, whose bloodshot eyes did he feel on his back, whose murderous gasps? And so, in the cold, silent, tenebrous church, before Her face, resound the footsteps, shouts and shots, reflections of ancient fires and flashes of distant explosions. The stir of the harbour where he wanders for the whole of December of that even more horrible year of 1919. In a worn–out army coat, the young Russian doctor, officer of the defeated army, rambles through Odessa, thinking of his beloved who is far away, of his home which is no longer his. We can see him on 26th January, 1919, boarding an old and decrepit French ship bearing the famous name of Patras. We can see him on a sorry piece of scrap iron, packed with despair and people with hollow eyes. With the collar pulled up, he watches the waves and surges of the rough winter sea, understanding nothing. Perhaps another member of the White Guard, Ivan Alekseyevich Bunin, is very near, imprinting onto his memory: *Suddenly I was completely awake, in a moment it dawned on me: Yes, this is it – I am on the Black Sea, on a foreign ship sailing God knows why to Istanbul, Russia is finished, and so is everything else, my past life is finished, even if another miracle happens and I do not drown in this malicious and icy sea...* We can see him in Istanbul with the domes of Hagia Sophia in the background, which people dreamt about in the holy cities of Russia and, thinking of them, erected orthodox crosses. And true enough, the Tsarist Army did come to the holy city, and Semyonov was with it; but he is only an insignificant part of the huge, confused, frightened crowd. Everything is terrible, and the world is coming to an end. But, he is alive, and twenty–five years old. He has left behind the face of death, before him are the cities of Bulgaria and Greece, the incense of Serbian churches, the suburbs of foreign, indifferent

14

European capitals. Others are staying, they gather in groups, but Semyonov does not stop. Wherever they are, his brothers, there is also the breath of ruthless pursuers. When a turbulence in the whirl which will, years later, scatter crowds of Russians around Europe, throws him into this region, he suddenly discovers this chapel in a European nook which cannot be found on any known map. To live again, without thinking of escape and return, never again to run or return anywhere. To live among these peasants, like a Tolstoy, to survive. Moments of fear and despair return when the emigres come to visit him from the town, conversations, mother Russia, insane illusions; he is relieved when Fedyatin's Rasputin–like shadow disappears into the cold morning. There will be no more flight, no repetition of the terrible 1918 and even more terrible 1919. Naively, with all his heart, he trusts in the mercy bestowed upon him. When the roaring of the Red Army is heard from the distance, Semyonov for the first time senses the horror of a huge, absurd misunderstanding.

Time and space are falling apart. The shadows of the flickering candle flame are running over her face. Over her eyes, gazing into the darkness and across the river. The thousands of kilometres that he has travelled, and the long years that he has survived, everything is disintegrating between the shadows. Suddenly, he is again exactly where he was once before. At the beginning, at the starting point. Twenty–seven years older and alone, he is standing in a cold church. He is looking for a sign in her eyes, to explain or help him understand. He feels icy cold in his chest and a deadly silence telling him that he is forsaken by Her and God, Her son, that there are no years behind him and no memories. With cold anxiety he discerns the mysterious and somewhat ironic hand of fate, which did not bring him here to save him and put a full stop to his flight. It brought him here solely to record a different version of the story which once had a happy ending. In the meantime fate had been dozing, letting him live for twenty–seven years, and today, on 16th May, 1945, began a new paragraph with the words: It could have ended differently, in that moment between life and death, everything could have been resolved differently.

The candles have burnt out, and in meagre morning light Vladimir Semyonov still gazes at the immobile face of Mary–of–the–Snows.

On 17th May, 1945, at dawn, Vladimir Semyonov comes out of the church. His face is waxen and twisted with derangement. He stops on the hill among the crosses. Among the crosses on the hill at Mary–of–the–Snows stands a Russian White Guardsman, looking over the landscape with empty eyes. Down there is the river and behind it a wide plain, gentle mist creeping over it. For a long time he cannot avert his eyes from the silent morning landscape across the river. There is no sound, no roaring. Everything is silent and hollow, like a deep, endless abyss. *There exists a force which sometimes tempts us to look over the edge of a precipice, which lures us down into the emptiness.* An hour later, a girl approaches him, carrying bright and clanging milk cans. The Russian doctor does not return the greeting, as if he could neither see nor hear her. Then he stands by the river, through the willows watching the fast and dark water. His blind eyes awaken when he hears voices on the other bank. The roaring river becomes silent, the mist thinner, when he hears the voices of the two figures on the other side. They linger around in grey coats, rifles on their shoulders with fixed bayonets. The first steps to the water and Vladimir Semyonov can distinctly and clearly see him as he speaks out: Posmotri, reka kakaja tjomnaja... mutnaja. At first he feels something warm and familiar and gentle overcome him, he would like to go over there and hug them for having finally come. Then he sees the other one pick up a stone and throw it into the river, he can see him answer: Ona njet mutnaja. Ona takaja glubokaja... očen tjomnaja potomu čto glubokaja. Now he finally realizes that he has taken a step too many towards the abyss, and down, into nothingness. He sees nothing more, he can only hear himself ascending the hill, his loud panting and beating in the temples. His mad flight, which is frantically beginning again, or perhaps simply continuing, so that he no longer knows whether it is 1918 again or what, whether he is here or somewhere else. And then he suddenly stops. A sharp and clear thought cuts through him like a blade. He shall run no more, he shall haul no more hope along. He can travel another thousand kilometers and live another twenty–seven years. But just before the end he will return to where everything began, in an empty and timeless moment between life and death.

Then he went upstairs and put a bullet through his temple. He had a steady officer's and doctor's hand, for the bullet only made a small hole and left behind a thick drip of blood which poured down his waxen face.

The Russian doctor, Vladimir Semyonov, was found around eleven in the morning by the mowers who came to collect their promised wages. The laid him on the bed and crossed themselves. The young men respected the presence of death, but nevertheless they looked around for something to take as payment for the work done in good faith. As they fumbled around in their peasant awkwardness, they overturned and broke the framed old icon which stood on a cabinet. One of them took nothing. He was the boy who, with cold beads of sweat on his forehead, once tried to kiss the doctor's hand. And yet it was he who, unintentionally, with a dirty sole, stepped on the icon, on the golden beads above Her eyes.

...

People who liked the strange Russian doctor, despite all the love, later said that he had committed a great stupidity. And if stupidity was too harsh a word for death and such a sad end, then at least, according to them, he had committed an unbelievably pointless act. Everyone knew that the soldiers of the Red Army in grey coats never crossed the river, they stayed on the other bank. Everyone knew it but him. Let us forgive them these words, for our naive human mind is not driven by reason, but by infinite hope. And therefore, a simple human conclusion cannot take into account the possibility that everything was determined in advance, a long time ago, and that fate perhaps wanted exactly this denouement. We can complain about its cruel pranks, the irony and senselessness of its second version, but fate chose the ending, it left Semyonov to lie with warm blood pouring down his waxen face, and there is nothing we can do about it. It is common knowledge that this mysterious lady writes the literature which again and again places insoluble riddles before us. She can see beyond our vision. We can only see to the other side of the river, and not always, as this story proves.

17

THE JUMP OFF THE LIBURNIA

Jump. He was standing about a metre from the edge. The dark surface below was moving rapidly. He was standing about a metre from the edge of the side of the ship, with one hand holding the rail at his back, looking at the water surface quickly moving past, his other hand swayed, and with it his slightly bent body. Jump, she said.

It was night, the shell of the sky closed by clouds above, the dark surface below. Perhaps it vibrated slightly, perhaps it moved along the sides of the ship like the back of a big animal. In the air there was the smell of smoke which trailed from the wide muzzle of the funnel above them. There was no wind, but the smoke was nevertheless being pushed downwards, so that from time to time he felt its sharp smell in his nostrils, mixed with the fragrance of water, possibly of salt. Jump, she said, and her quiet, careless voice cut through the middle of his body, and settled on top of his stomach. He could feel that something was actually drawing him down, into the depths. The feeling had emerged a moment before, maybe a minute before, a minute before he jumped over the rail and took a step away from her, towards the dark, rapidly moving abyss. A minute before he had been stretched on a deck chair, his feet by the edge of the rail; a minute before he had been smoking a cigarette. A minute before he had tossed the burning cigarette end over the rail, he had watched the flashing dot hang in the darkness for a moment, sway, and then draw a bright arc downwards. It seemed to him that he could hear a hiss on the surface. Of course, nothing hissed, nothing could be heard apart from the smooth hum of the ship's engine. It only disappeared; something, which a moment before had been in his hands had disappeared completely and finally, and after what had disappeared nothing was left, neither in the air, nor in the water, nor in the darkness in which the ship's depths were sunk. Into which they were both sunk, stretched in canvas deck chairs at the side of the ship, after dinner, without speaking, with vacant eyes staring into the darkness towards where the shore was supposed to be, where the shore actually was, since twinkling lights emerged there and disappeared again, on the shore, perhaps deep inland.

– Say it again, he said.

He tore his gaze from the lights on the shore and felt rather than saw the dark surface of the sea, the deep plane, his heart started beating faster. The feeling which lay on top of his stomach rose towards his heart, towards the hollow inside, towards the hammering in the middle of the body's hollow space, and the dangerous, frightened thought whizzed through his brain that he might actually jump; if she said it just once more he would have no strength left to step back. She must feel it, this is not a game any more. If only a moment before, when he had followed the cigarette end with his eyes, when he had stood up and climbed over the metal rail, if it had all been a prank, then now, suddenly, everything was at stake. She must feel he is being drawn into the abyss, she must get up and hug him, she must at least be quiet. She was quiet. But it was not enough any more. Let her feel the fear running through him, for God's sake, let her be humiliated only for a moment, let her beg him, ask him to move. Why is she lying behind his back motionless, wrapped in a blanket, why does she not with a single gesture put a stop to all the misunderstandings which have accumulated during the last few years in their lives? Let her utter just one word and the sudden madness will be cured, they will both be cured. He could feel that in this long moment she was probably thinking, judging his readiness for risk, it seemed to him that she had moved. She must get up, she must say a word, this will be a word of concern for him, a word of love and salvation. Let her at least say, you are behaving like a child; let her say, stop this nonsense; let her say, it's cold, let's go down into the cabin; let her say, the water is cold, let her make a joke, let her laugh, let her cough, let her yawn. He let go of the rail and his hands hung by his body, he bent his head. Where is the froth, is it behind the ship? Where are the waves, have they been swallowed up by the dark? He could feel her breathing behind his back, her eyes fixed on his nape. They were alone, a few young people were asleep in their sleeping bags, sheltered from the wind at the bow of the ship, no body could be seen, no hand or head, stretched, withered corpses, wrapped in silky textile. Say a single word, he thought, and you will be forgiven everything, I will be forgiven everything, everything we have done to each other in recent years; I'm sorry for everything, I'm really sorry, just say a word, he thought. This is not humiliation, or, is it humiliation if you take a step towards me, a single step? After so many years of marriage, after so many wounds, just a word; say, this is a silly provocation; say, one shouldn't play with things like this, shouldn't stand at the edge of the ship, shouldn't look down. Down into the intoxicating, crazily intoxicating depth which wants to draw one to itself, flatten one on itself, pull, sink to the dark bottom.

– Jump, she said.

My God, he thought, my God, now I'll really jump. Actually, I'll just take a step forward, a step too many. Now I really feel dizzy, he thought. Now he can no longer think, what a horrible provocation, what has actually happened, why is he standing here being drawn over the edge, he cannot think of anything, everything has gone quiet – the ship and the engine, the beating of his heart in his chest and head, only the echo of the silence is left. He stepped to the very edge and swayed dangerously, I'm a good swimmer, he thought nevertheless, at fifty I'm still a good swimmer; will the siren blow, will I be pulled under the ship? It seemed to him that she had got up. He desperately turned round, she had not got up. In the corner of his eye he caught the dishevelled head of a stranger, she poked it from the sleeping bag, the startled eyes of a girl. A mouse out of flour, he thought and clung to the thought, a mouse out of flour; why do we say a mouse out of flour, how does a mouse look out of flour, what has a mouse looking out of flour to do with that dishevelled head, with the sleepy astonished unknown girl's eyes looking out of a sleeping bag? There's nothing I can say, I'll jump now, I'll step over the edge and a moment later it'll be all over. I can't do anything, I mustn't say anything, everything is hollow and quiet and crazily frightened, and yet decided. Say nothing.

– I'm saying it for the last time, he said, say it for the last time.

Because of the gaze, transfixed by the dark running surface, the depth, because of the magnetism drawing him down, because of the something with no name, his body started trembling. What is it, he thought, am I drunk? They had drunk a bottle of wine with dinner. Will I swim out? I'm not drunk, I won't swim out. The thought was looking for an exit in fast, energetic thrusts. The sea is the Adriatic, the ship is the Liburnia, we are man and wife, many years at the edge, now I'm standing at the edge, in the distance, on the shore, there is light, the depths are dark, the ship is wrapped in darkness. Sometimes, when he stood on the tower by the pool, on a rock by the sea, when the tiny boy's shuddering body, the frightened trembling soul, wanted to show his friends that he dared, that he really dared, he used to count, count to three, and then he always jumped: when he started counting he knew he would jump, although he knew there would be terrible moments of absence during the fall, that it might hurt down below, the impact on the surface. Now it was different, everything was the same, but nevertheless different. The point now was to spring into the heart, not into the sea, his heart and hers, the heart in which everything began and acquired its sense. But to accomplish this she must utter a word, a single word, it must not be a humiliating word, it must not be the ironic: jump, it must not be: jump–because–of–me, it must not be his failure at this edge, this moment, can she not feel it in her chair, wrapped in a blanket, this moment life can start anew. This moment his body is trembling, can she not perceive it, this moment he is really irresistibly being drawn to the depths. The brief laughter of young people drifted from the deck, a door slammed, a discarded bottle rushed past in the sea, the dome of the cloudy sky lowered. He

21

felt his palms were sweaty, beads of cold sweat emerged on his forehead, cold wind started blowing and again he could feel the stinking smoke from the ship in his nostrils. Will this be the end, the last sensory perceptions he will take over the edge, into the emptiness, into the dark? Or will she now say a word, another word?

I'm saying it for the last time, he said, say it for the last time. He said it twice, it was like counting to three in his boyhood years, he said it twice, at short intervals he answered quickly, angrily, challengingly, humiliatingly, now is three, a moment later I say three, I'm saying it for the last time, he said, say it for the last time.

– Jump, she said quietly.

She said it quietly, she said it with a quieter voice, and this stopped him for a moment. But at the same instant the thought caught up with the brain that she had said it, said it despite everything, she had said what she should not have said for anything in the world, and he sprang over the edge. Actually, he did not spring, he had no strength left for that. He simply took a step forward, he simply moved his foot and collapsed into the dark empty space. To tell the truth, he did not step into the deep void, he slipped into it. He sat at the edge, clutched the metal frame with his hands and slid along the edge towards the rapidly approaching, larger and larger, more and more painful surface of the sea.

No ground under the feet, nothing to hold on to, he flew through space, through the dissolved and supple airy matter. The cloudy dome of the sky and the blue–black surface of the sea were turned upside-down and united, now the sky was below, then it was carried away and blurred, now something gradually rose in his chest, then his heart was captured by its own trembling which at the same time was the trembling of the air through which he flew. Everything was visible and yet invisible, the direction of the fall was simultaneously up and down, the curve of the horizon was rounded, gravity was derailed, the unity of the world became denser and at the same time open, the water and the air, the sea and the sky. The bodily matter disintegrated on contact with the immobile surface of the sea. For a moment he could see the light on the shore towards which he was supposed to swim, for an instant he saw the immense shadow of the ship, its metal side, its dark body rushing past, dragging him towards it. He heard a scream, a shrill when he heard the roaring of the ship engines, their coughing and stopping, the grumbling signal siren; when he heard it all he was far behind, in the middle of the spuming waves the monster was leaving behind, far below without vision or hearing, without breathing or pain, enclosed in the watery matter, the disappearance, the prenumbness.

She was still lying wrapped in a blanket, now, by the white metal wall, in the dark. She lifted her head only slightly. The girl with the dishevelled hair and mousey, tiny, sleepy eyes lit a cigarette. She raised her head only slightly to see him more clearly clutching the metal rail, murmuring something into his chin. He did not swing himself over the edge, he did not move his foot and with a single step fall into the void, he did not slide along the side of the ship towards the rapidly approaching, larger and larger, more and more painful surface of the sea.

He did not jump. He did not spring into the centre, the heart, the place where everything began and acquired its sense. He did not throw himself anywhere. He stood by the rail and felt that his trembling body was calming down, that the hollow void in his head and chest was filling with noises, senses, looks. The ship alone was shuddering with the jolts of the engine, the sharp, stinking smoke was filling his nostrils, he looked towards the shore and watched the approaching lights of a town. I'll hit you, he thought, I'll kill you. Down in the cabin, if not here, then down in the cabin.

– How could you, he said, how could you?

A warm wind started blowing from the shore. The lights of the town were approaching. If he had turned he would have seen that, despite the warm wind from the shore, she had pulled the blanket up to her chin. If he had turned he would have seen there was nevertheless a hint of surprise and uncertainty in her eyes. Not fear, simply uncertainty and surprise. This would have sufficed. But he did not turn.

– What does Liburnia actually mean? she said quietly.

He was silent. How could you, how could you?

– You don't know? he said. It was an ancient Illyrian kingdom, you don't know.

– It's cold, she said after a while, let's go down.

It was not cold, it was warm, warm wind blew from above the stony hills, with piles of stones on top, ancient Illyrian graves. There it probably roared and howled around the peaks, from there it blew clouds above the water, here it dissolved into a soft mass of air above the sea surface which was suddenly no longer an oily quiet surface but a slightly wrinkled one, with frothy crests in places. The girl in the sleeping bag drew a few more puffs from the cigarette, then she threw the burning end over the rail, into the dark. The wind held it for a while, then forcibly carried it along the side of the ship, back and down. The dishevelled hair disappeared, she zipped up the sleeping bag over her head.

– Let's go down, he said. Let's go this time.

ULTIMA CREATURA

H ad Franc Rutar, on a humid afternoon long past, not fixed his gaze on the large letters of a book the woman sitting next to him was holding on her knees, everything would have ended much better. He would not have experienced the horrible things, which, even years later, when he thought of them with a mixture of painful discomfort and fear, appeared like images from some bad dreams. From moments between sleep and wakefulness. But he knew that this was not a dream, although everything had happened in a large, distant city, the pictures of which, just like dreams, were coming into his life from the TV screen. In the middle of a humid afternoon he was rushing into the underground, and the god he met there was black and dreadful. At least, he claimed he was God, and Franc Rutar recognized him as such, although then and even now he thought he had been somebody else, God's dark antithesis. God does not think of such cheap tricks, he does not seek weak points in the weak moments of settled people in such a way. Franc Rutar was more and more certain of this, the more distant the unpleasant event became.

Sales representative, Franc Rutar, was an avaricious reader. Although numbers and letters often danced before his tired eyes, he could not help swallowing every single word and letter that happened to be in his field of vision. He was one of those people who, in waiting rooms, in buses or just anywhere read from newspapers and books that were not theirs. They cannot help glancing at the front page of the paper somebody else holds in their hands. Many do it out of laziness and tightness, some out of thievish impulses: they read over the owner's shoulder, and since they know very well how annoying this is, they always look away just before they are caught red-handed, and start looking through the windows or at the tips of their shoes. Some of these readers never even think of the fact that they are actually stealing somebody else's property with their eyes, letter by letter, like bits of a female body, like bread from a table. Franc Rutar could not complain of a scarcity of his foreign trade and other reading material. However, reading the papers and books other people held in their hands became his uncontrollable passion. By doing it, he again and again tested his exact mind; Franc Rutar was a man with an exact mind and perfect memory. He immediately connected the dancing titles and fragments of pages into rounded logical wholes; a sports report was never mixed up with a political one. Anyone who has an orderly head can apprehend the order of the world, and mistakes cannot happen. His greatest pleasure was to catch a glimpse of a crossword puzzle; he could feel pins and needles at the sudden challenge and risk. He could test the speedy operation of his brain, which was one of his greatest assets in concluding risky editorial deals; rapid considerations, swift decisions. With brisk calculations, tossing the words around, he managed to solve the puzzles between two stops. Franc Rutar was of the opinion, according to his own beliefs, that he was one of the supreme achievements of the Creation.

On the very first day he proved this fact to the colleague from his company with whom he had come to New York. After a few hours of his stay in the metropolis he understood the mathematics of Manhattan streets, finding them no more difficult than the average crossword puzzle. Thanks to him they were able to quickly carry out sophisticated foreign trade deals. On the third day he felt at home in this human anthill of business, he beamed at his friend's praise; that was the famous dexterity and ingenuity of Franc Rutar's mind, he did not lack reasons for satisfaction.

Not even after he had, on the third afternoon of his stay – it was a stuffy afternoon, saturated with ocean humidity – appeased his hunger with cheap fried chicken in a fast-food restaurant. He contentedly sat on a subway train, which was to take him somewhere towards Battery Park, where he wanted to take a walk around Wall Street. He was in New York, his business settled, his stomach full, the world was high and life beautiful. But when the world is at its highest, the fall from the top is deepest.

He looked around him for an open newspaper. He was going to test his impeccable English in the risky game of connecting fragments into logical wholes, between two stops. He was about to get up to step behind the back of a man holding a folded paper in one hand and clutching on to the swaying handle with the other, when a better, for the moment of contentment more appropriate opportunity arose. A beautiful coloured girl sat down next to him, actually a woman, a girl still, but a woman at the same time. She opened a book on her lap, and was absorbed in reading. There was no need to stretch his neck, no need to stand behind somebody's back and look over a shoulder, luxurious reading was right there, immobile, open above the round, chocolate-brown knees. The letters were large, so he could easily follow the text written in simple English. The task was almost too simple. But he had just come from lunch, warm matter, mixed with fried Kentucky chicken, was lazily and happily flowing through his body. He abandoned himself to the large letters and the rocking train rushing into the black underground.

He suddenly felt excited and wide awake. The text resting on top of the naked chocolate knees, nicely cooled in the subway in the middle of a stuffy day above, was shocking. Franc Rutar had never read anything like it, at least not in a train: a young woman was just about to lie, half way through the left page of the book, with an older man, actually an old man, as it soon became clear. It was written in the first person, the narrator was the woman. She locked the door of her flat behind her, she was undoing the buttons on his shirt, at the beginning of the following page she leaned towards his neck and with intoxicated desire was smelling his aged skin.

27

Franc Rutar deeply resented any frivolity, temptations of the flesh, and contacts with strangers were in opposition to the order in his mind. He avoided all the things that some of his colleagues openly looked for on business trips. He once looked at the women in shop-windows in Hamburg, but to spend his hard earned money on them never crossed his mind, not even in a dream. However, before the impulse reached his mind, he was all in a trembling frenzy he had never experienced before. Was it the humid day or was it the inconceivable fact that the young woman, who was not even a woman yet, was sitting next to him and reading such things? Also the sudden decision that he would not get off and finish the story in his mind, but that he would, on the contrary, actually read the thing on the knees, was spontaneous; it was not the product of consideration, but of some unknown impulse in his brain and body. Voraciously he read the next page, on which the senseless erotic scene continued, and he could only conclude that the girl in the book was either intoxicated, crazy or in love in some strange way. He waited impatiently for the slow reader to turn the page. He had long moments at his disposal to take a better look at her. He saw her moving lips. Moist, red lips. He missed his stop, but she still had not turned the page. She was moving her knees. A naive girl, he thought, she is embellishing her life with cheap romances in large type. She must work in one of those department stores, wrapping up clothes with awkward fingers all day long. He thought he would get off after all. At that moment the round chocolate knees moved, she put one leg over the other, and turned the page at the same time. Everything happened simultaneously, for a long moment her hot thigh pressed against his with such strength that something rushed from his brain and his sex into his chest at the same time, whizzed towards his heart and there, above the top of his stomach, this hollow something settled down and refused to dissolve. The letters started twinkling before his eyes.

He did not get off. He heard the roaring of the train rushing somewhere into the underground.

She lifted the covers, and through the mist of his stunned eyes he saw on the fluorescent red cover the hollow between the woman's breasts, a broken necklace above them, crystal drops of sweat or water. The title of the book he read in a split second was: The World Is Full of Married Men. Whatever was holding a grip on his heart loosened, and what lay hollow on top of his stomach dissolved. He flinched, and his exact brain started working with computer speed, so that something cracked with fatigue a few times just under the arch of his skull. This here, he thought, this here is a set-up. This girl, his precise mind continued, is sitting on the subway just for this. The letters are so large so that somebody else can read them, under the book, chocolate knees. Yet, his mind crackled in an effort: Why? It is done differently for money. Because, his quick brain answered, because the girl wants to experience exactly this. She is coloured, discriminated against, frustrated. Where else can she find a businessman, an older man, even an aged man, if not on the subway? She might become his mistress; it is common knowledge that this kind of man in their most secret dreams want unpredictable events, young mulatto girls. At this conclusion he again became pleased with himself, although not a bit less excited; if he had been merely excited a few minutes before, and before that only pleased, then now he was both, excited and pleased. Excited flesh, contented mind. She had sat down next to him, not somebody else. It was true that his belly was growing and that he had a monkish tonsure on his head, although it was not showing. He must still have been immensely more interesting than the old man described with such passion on the strange pages of the book resting on the knees. I'll get off, he decided, where she gets off, and let happen what must. One can, after all, take a ride back the very next moment. He was astonished by such a brisk decision. If she asks for money, he thought, and prolonged the thought into a consideration, I can think about that on the spot. He was pleased with himself, the decision originated from his reason and contentment, partly from excitement.

The train was at that moment scurrying towards Brooklyn. We're traveling under the water, he thought, what an adventure, up there is the huge, dark mass of the bridge we know from films; he, Franc Rutar is riding underneath it, a coloured girl is seducing him. He was looking at her knees, the rim of her skirt above them, he was touching her ribs under the light blouse with his elbow, his gaze fixed on her dark skin, he was traveling into her. Derma, his brain quickly said, five letters from a crossword puzzle. What's the matter with me, he thought, where am I going?

She stood up and smoothed her skirt. He stepped to the door, close behind her. He straightened his tie and thought it would soon be undone, just like the one on the pages of the book she was now clutching under her sweaty arm. On the platform she looked straight into his eyes, he felt the look penetrated deeply. No, there was no doubt about it. His heart was pounding. All he needed to do now was find the courage to address her. It would not happen without speaking. He was rapidly searching for words. He would speak in a muffled way, slightly through the nose, to conceal his Slovene accent. Her hips were swaying in front of his eyes, the light from the street approached and a house with a shabby facade above it. He would speak loudly, so that she would not be able to hear the hammering of his heart. Before they reached the top he had found the right words. Interesting book, isn't it? he said. What? she laughed with her pearl- white teeth, What? The book, he said through his nose, with a deep voice. Oh yes, the book, she said and laughed brightly. He youthfully jumped over a few steps, now they were in the street. Again he was at a loss for words in the empty space in his skull. He found them. May I buy you a coffee? he said with an even deeper voice. I could buy you one, she said, so that he did not know whether it was an invitation or an ironic refusal. If you came this far, the suddenly determined brain said, then go all the way. Or maybe it said nothing. The sales representative, Franc Rutar, probably because of everything unexpected that had happened in his life was left without the brain which had helped him to conclude business transactions and solve crossword puzzles so successfully. If he had still had the brain, he would have seen that he was accompanying a young black woman at a fast pace along a horribly shabby New York street, jumping over heaps of rubbish and avoiding bodies lying on the sidewalks. Through black people sitting on steps, through their faces he pushed his way after her, after her all the time, through a door into a dark hall. From there new stairs led high up, between wooden walls close together. Through a narrow corridor, up the steep stairs he walked close behind her, with no eyes, with the smell of her derma in his nostrils, with his sweat pouring through his hair, dripping from his forehead and slithering into his shirt; with the smell of rotten wood which was covered in places with peeling wallpaper.

At the top she opened a door, then another. They were in a small room. Children's chatter was coming from the street, and tenants' echoing calls from balconies and windows, and wild musical confusion from different directions. In the corner, in semi darkness stood a shabby couch with a metal spring sticking from it. He loosened his tie, although he still expected her to do it before undoing the buttons on his shirt, as it was done in the book. Sweat was pouring from his face, his heart was pounding crazily, partly because of the run up the stairs. In a corner of his mind, not the one with swift and precise thoughts, but the one with a premonition, something said something; he could not discern what exactly it said, it did not run along the folds, it did not switch itself on, and even if it had, if he could have discerned what that something was which had said something, and what it had said, it would have been too late.

The dark girl sat on the couch in the dark part of the room, she looked emptily at the wall, opened her mouth and started screaming. Surprised, he looked at the disfigured face of the being sitting there, and he could not understand why, why she was sitting there screaming; he thought of somehow stopping that open mouth, from which a high, monotonous shriek was coming. Excuse me, he said, this is a misunderstanding, he said, I'm sorry. I'll hit her, he thought, why is she screaming, I haven't done anything to her, I'll hit her, he thought.

She did not scream long, towards the end not even very loudly. The door opened immediately. A young black man walked in, with a massive gold chain around his neck. He was chewing negligently. What's going on here? he said, he mumbled the question rather indistinctly, and it must have meant what Franc Rutar had already understood: he was her protector. He wanted to rape me, the girl said, as she would have said It's four in the afternoon. The chewing man looked at him accusingly and with surprise. Who? he asked. She pointed at Franc Rutar with her finger: Him.

At that moment his brain finally recognized what was coming from the vast premonition area. He was trapped. He thought he was a stupid, contented man, whose brain worked stupidly, following stupid instincts; suddenly he did not understand how he happened to be there at all. I'm, he said, by chance... It did not sound convincing. He was dripping with cold sweat, and he felt a strange emptiness spreading in his head, something completely unspecified, something like nothing. I'm sorry, he said, I'm sorry, and took a step towards the door. The black young man pressed his back against it. It was impossible to leave the place just like that. If muggers stop you in the street, his memory whispered to him, have a ten–dollar bill ready in your pocket. Give it to them immediately, without wasting any words. He reached into his breast pocket and discovered with relief that the money was still there. Franc Rutar was a careful man, ready for anything, even for being stopped in the street by hooligans. But he was not in a street. He was in an unknown flat, in an unknown part of town, the exit from this dive was blocked by a young man who was chewing and playing with the chain on his chest. He never even looked at the banknote, he opened the door and called somebody. Immediately two other men walked in, they obviously could not have been very far away. One of them took over the post by the door; the other, a tall and slender middle– aged man, walked around the room. He was wearing a white linen jacket, he exchanged a few sentences with the girl, who was still sitting by the protruding spring; he spoke Spanish. He then turned to Franc Rutar, who with eyes full of hope was following his movements and speech. He said they would call the police. Yes, the sales representative whispered, yes, the police. Everybody went quiet, the young and the tall one exchanged a long look. No, Franc Rutar said, no need to call. Sir, the young man with the chain said, Sir, your tie is undone. He lifted his chin and fastened his tie so tightly that he was left breathless. This doesn't make any sense, Franc Rutar thought, any sense. The tall man offered him a seat by the girl. He sank into himself and lowered his eyes. The tall man walked around the room and asked the girl questions, she answered with shrieking, bickering screams, the nauseating screech of the imagined girl with chocolate derma. The mumbling young man joined in the conversation, only the third one stood silently by the door. Oh my God, the sales rep thought, they are fighting for the prey. He was made to stand by the wall and raise his arms so that they were able to search him. Then he had to empty his pockets and since there was no table, put everything on the floor. The young man with the chain suddenly became very angry. The wallet was not among the articles on the floor. He shouted something incomprehensible, he turned round as if dancing, and hit Franc Rutar on the neck with his half–open fist so hard that he instantly collapsed on the floor. At once he handed him his wallet. The white jacket asked him something. He did not understand, he did not know what to answer. He grabbed his hair and shook his poor head and breathed his sweet breath into him. He could not, he did not understand, he did not know what was happening. Oh my dear Mamma, he muttered to himself, my dear Mummy, look what's happening to Franci. The girl opened his business case and emptied it on the couch. With clawing movements she scratched among his papers, put his pocket calculator and his glasses between the covers of the book; the tall one took the case. This is horrible, he thought, horrible what is happening to Franci far away from home; if his wife knew; he thought of everybody he loved who were so far away. But, what had happened so far was nothing in comparison with what followed.

He had to take his clothes off. He folded them on the couch. The third man, the one who was standing by the door without speaking, pulled a knife from his pocket, opened it, moved the blade down his neck. Then he lowered it to his sex. He'll cut it off, Franc Rutar realized, and put it in my mouth. The girl was frantically feeling his clothes. They were pushing him around the room and screaming over one another. Her shrieks were piercing his ears, the membrane of the tympanum, penetrating into the soft tissue of the brain. Somebody switched on the radio, somebody drank from a can, pouring beer all over him. The noise was terrible. Then for a moment there was silence in the room, through the veil of mist he saw a tall black man in a dark jacket approach. He came very close and quietly whispered into his ear, so that his head hollowly echoed with his breath and words. I'm your God, he said, do you understand? Franci nodded. Repeat, he said, repeat: who am I? God, he said, my God. Your great God, the tall black man said, his head was just below the ceiling when he stood up, Franc Rutar was lying on the floor, the small head of the great God high above. My great God, he said loudly, as many times as he could. He heard his voice getting lost in the empty space, coming back with an echo, as if he had been speaking in a huge hall.

He was forced to lie on the floor and put his hands on his nape. They walked around the room and again talked loudly. They stumbled over him, somebody sat on top of him for a moment. Now... he thought... the knife. Or... a blow on the head. He could see his corpse floating under Brooklyn bridge, the shadow of the giant bridge above, below, under the water, the rattling of the subway. He remembered he used to know a prayer, he started moving his trembling lips, pressed against the dirty wooden floor: Our Father who art in Heaven. The clamour was far away, the musical chaos was coming from yards and balconies. Darkness fell over his eyes, voices and words, screams and slams of the door became intermingled. His body became insensitive, black shadows danced around him. He shrank into a little boy being put into a cauldron and danced around. Now they'll cut me into pieces, the dreaming boy in the bed thought, and they'll put me into that cauldron, into that big vessel Mamma used to cook jam in. Then he knew he was asleep, and that he saw his white body floating under the bridge, in its large shadow. The belly was slightly swollen, the tumult of the city coming from afar. The tumult changed into a shrill, hissing noise. Steam was hissing from a pipe. Again he heard Spanish words from a distance, then they became Latin; was it the tall black man in the white jacket speaking? He could hear two words quite distinctly; from a crossword puzzle, said his brain, which was obviously still working, from a difficult puzzle. Ultima creatura, he said. Ultima creatura. He rapidly placed the letters in the squares, his inner eye saw the squares and the two emerging words. Do these black gods speak Latin? he thought with surprise; there is a certain logic in it, he thought, gods always speak Latin; is that what the black God is telling him?

For a long time he listened to the hissing of the steam, penetrating his awakening consciousness together with calls from the distance, from the street, probably from the balconies in the neighbouring buildings. He opened his eyes. It was dark in the room, a ray of light from the street fell at an angle onto his white body. In the empty flat, only then did he realize there was no glass in the windows, it smelt of humidity, decaying wallpaper, rotten wood. All his senses functioned: smell, sight, hearing, the aching body. There were holes in the floor, his clothes lay crumpled on it, in the corner a white, slovenly pile, the shirt, that was the shirt. The tie hung on the spring sticking from the pierced couch. He dressed. Feeling through the darkness he descended the steep stairs of the empty house.

He arrived at his hotel towards morning. He told no-one what had happened to Franci. To his friend who knocked on the door he said he had been robbed in a park. He did not find it necessary to explain anything. When the friend looked at him with surprise through the half-open door, looked at the deep scar running from the ear towards the mouth, he closed the door and lay on the bed. Explain nothing. Say nothing. Even think nothing. He did not leave the room until he left for home. He lay on the bed and lovingly looked at the plane ticket and the passport, which had been, on advice from the homeland, left locked in the hotel safe. The representative Franc Rutar was a careful and sensible man. At least he still had a tiny reason for satisfaction.

For many years he dreamt he was being put into that big vessel his Mamma used to cook jam in. He floated in the shadow of a huge bridge, with his belly white and swollen. In an empty room a black god leaned over him and breathed unknown horrible words into his ears. When the silhouette of an unknown city or bridge appeared on TV, he switched the set off and had a fight with his wife, who could not understand it. He always had it his way, he could not stand humiliation. He avoided young mulatto girls from department stores. Luckily, there were not

35

many in his country. Never again did he read over somebody else's shoulder or tackle a crossword puzzle.

A few years after the trip to New York, on a winter night, by the fence of his suburban house, he knocked down a drunken tramp who had asked him for some change. Creature, he shouted, creature, and kicked the rasping heap on the ground. He was in the local paper, which discretely published only his initials: R.R. That was all, nothing else happened apart from the things that happen to anyone of us.

BRANE GRADIŠNIK

Translated by the author

Brane Gradišnik, born 1951 in Ljubljana. Studied history of art and sociology at Ljubljana University and took his M.A. degree in creative writing at the University of Lancaster. He published three books of short stories, a suspense story 'The Other Man', 1990, and a novel 'Lethe', 1985. Apart from being a fiction and script-writer, he translates, mostly from English (G.K. Chesterton, P. Pearce, A.A. Milne, R. Adams, M. Twain, K. Vonnegut, J.M. Cain, R. Ellison, J. Dickey).

OEOPATH

I'm writing this in utter peace, reconciled with myself and with the enormous possibilities life imposes. Senses cannot deceive me any more: it's a glass of sweet southern wine awaiting me at my elbow, it's a fly crawling over my instep, it's a breeze that the olive–trees are quivering their twigs in. Yes, yes, and I can hear, as if through a drowse, bathers calling to each other down at the shore. There's something in the air that announces a tempest by nightfall, maybe it's the haziness of sounds, or the white of the sky, immobile and quiet, but there is time enough, I think, to jot down into a story all that was once real, even if it now seems an illusion. This is the earth, my planet, my world, shimmering, smoothly moving into the future: the meadow, now yellowed by the cicada grating, later blue in dusk, the piling of the clouds, the swish of the first sprays of gale, the joyful screams of fire–kindlers running under the cover of their tents, the pureness of the washed air, the flicker of fireflies and the coming of the dawn.

It wasn't so long ago when, on a completely different afternoon, I was returning from the office, walking close to the houses to evade the spell of the many eyes and touches. Nevertheless, I couldn't help seeing an old lady nearly run down by a silent car. And a stray dog waiting for the green light. And a cross–eyed street–sweeper who had crept out of his usual night cover, trying to pin and pick up and store in his two–wheeled dustbin a crumpled manila envelope. At that moment, such powerful sounds reverberated from the window of a derelict attic that I could recognize the tune breaking through the traffic, and even if I forgot it after a hundred steps (yes, I was counting my steps) I still knew something inevitably unpleasant was about to happen. I swerved into a bar and ordered a glass of brandy. An old man was there. He was repeatedly trying to raise a glass to his mouth – his hand moving as if possessed, too jerkily for a robot, too mechanically for a man – and the drink finally spilled over the floor, drowned in layers of deepening gloom. And when I wanted to sip, I smelled a trace of urine in my glass, either because five weeks of abstaining had spoiled my sense of scent or because I had forgotten how it really smelled. Or maybe it was the other man, just staggering out of the toilet. I thought of smoking a cigarette, but then I felt a surge of fear that it would slip through my fingers. The intensity of this fear was exaggerated out of all proportion. It was the immobilizing fear of a field mouse caught by the swish of a night bird. It was... It was the fear... The fear itself. (I can use similes now, sitting among the olive-trees, but they weren't around when I needed them.) Finally I put the untouched drink aside and walked out, but at the doorstep I paused and said, "How can I say it's none of my business? How do I know that I won't end as a wretched wino whose nerves won't respond? That a car won't run me down? Some day I could still become a father, it is quite feasible. Would I wreak my anger on him, on my son, like this?" I was watching a worn-out woman jerkily pulling a crying child by the hand, trying to tear him off the traffic sign in front of me. Where were they heading? To the doctor? The dentist, or for a vaccination? Or were they going just to try on some clothes, to buy shoes, or to pay a visit to some unpleasantly loving auntie with golden molars? Children are so unsure, they cling to their bodies, nobody is to touch them, nobody to reach into what they feel is them. I stood there and watched the unpleasant scene from the edge of the rush. Finally, she tore the child off and dragged him through the gate at my right, where stone lions were squatting on a pair of cornerstones. It seemed to me that the child was limping. I was still looking after them, wondering whether they were headed to the orthopedist, when I felt the ripples of someone's gaze on the contracting skin of my nape. I quickly threw my glance around and met the steady, pale eyes of a grey-haired man in front of the next shop-window. He was standing as still as the mannequins at his back. What was the thing in me that had attracted his gaze in the same way the child's recalcitrance had attracted mine? And what was in him that made him look at me the way I had looked at the child? Uncertain, I stepped under the arch, between the lions. The entrance-hall was drenched with the sweet-sour smell of urine and I could see the map of its salt-like, overlapping layers under my feet. I made twenty steps through this hall littered with paper and orange peels, towards the directory at the opposite wall that promised, with its gold letters on black glass, more respectable interior further on, but when I came near I saw the glass was dusty and smudgy and cracked. All those men of learned professions, lawyers and architects and general practitioners, had moved out, leaving the place to cheap dressmakers and hosiers and piano-teachers whose cardboard, hand-written signs, thumbtacked to the wall more to the right, I perceived now, upon coming closer. Where was the child? Was he still crying? All I could hear was the traffic outside. I turned right and went through a green swinging door. Beneath, I found a smaller vestibule with stairs running upwards to the right. To the left, there were two rows of letter-boxes on the wall, mostly broken-in or gaping, some blackened by burnt-out mail. I knew there was nothing I could find there, but my sense of duty made me go through the boxes. Ordinary, criss-crossed or faded names. Dirty graffitos. An old, yellowed newspaper stuck into a box. Some uncollected council bills. There were sixteen boxes. When I came to the last one, I perceived a flight of narrow stairs at the far end of the vestibule. They led downwards. There was another cardboard sign, tacked askew to the flaking wall, and its red arrow was pointing towards the gloomy basement at the bottom of the staircase. Under the arrow I saw an Italian name, and underneath there was a strange word, presumably denoting a medical practitioner of some kind.

RAPATONI
OEOPATH
-12 NOON
7 PM

Coming closer, I found out that the sign had been torn. Some letters and numbers on the left side were missing. Oeopath – like an outcry of foreign, perhaps Greek sorrow. It could well be that the child was there, already becalmed by the oeopath's cure. Going down the stairs, I tentativelly tried to supplement the word, but the agglomeration of its initial vowels was too strange to graft any sense on it. I suppose I would have found another, clarifying sign in the basement, on Rapatoni's (or Trapatoni's?) door, but only a moment before getting to the bottom of the stairs I heard someone's easy steps from above coming nearer and then stopping short. It was after this moment of suspense, with my left footstill poised in the air above the penultimate step, with my right wrist gently touching the wall, that I finally lost my composure. The vision of the grey man descending upon me in this claustrophobic place and cornering me between his watery gaze and the oeopath's door was so frightening that I couldn't stop even after I had rushed past the delivery boy scratching his head by the letter–boxes, and plunged onto the street devoid, as I found out with one sweep of my gaze, of the old man's eyes.

My wife wasn't at home. We had become accustomed to live each for ourselves, or better, we had never got into the habit of living as a couple. She was an employee of the Red Cross Society and thus she could always get away from home. Yes, what in the world was she to do at home, where she was received by solitude, and unwashed dishes, and soil left on the floor by my garden boots, and eternal dust on the junior set of gay–coloured furniture which a rash uncle had given us as a wedding present and which we, with equally imprudent eagerness, had put into one of the rooms, so that I still had no library? During the last years, I used to spent my afternoons in the garden at the back of the house, digging, trimming, weeding, splitting. I enjoyed touching the soil, kneading it, warm and somehow alive. I enjoyed watching the budding of the unconscious life coming out of it in response to the sun and water and my hands. Sometimes I imagined my wife looking at me through the bluish haze of the evening, hidden behind the kitchen curtain and wondering how could I spend my time bent over this queer, solitary work, no longer advancing at my job, no longer striving. But later, retreating from the night cold into the house, I found the kitchen and the chairs empty, the curtains parted, the stew on the table cold. I didn't really care, because all this had come to pass so slowly and imperceptibly that it seemed natural, like the process of aging itself; and it was much easier than the tears, convulsions, door–slamming and suppressed thoughts of the early years. Therefore the empty house seemed to me normal until, going through my mail, I found two letters among the usual bills and statements. The blue one was stamped, but I couldn't decipher the smudgy postmark. The other one was a plain unsealed envelope, addressed in my wife's tidy handwriting. As I remember, I was briefly surprised also by the fact that the handwriting of the letters differed so much. The same calligraphic canon is applied in every school, but how is it then possible that our writing gets so varied afterwards? I put on the apron and the boots.

The last of the sun glistened on the grass. My neighbour was watering his lawn and at the far end of the spraying spurt, over the hedge, I suspected a rainbow. I sat down on a bench, took out from under it the garden–shears, and cut the edge of the posted letter. It was written by a long–forgotten friend who had returned from abroad and was now informing me that he was settling down in the near–by seaside resort. He was jocular. He mentioned some incidents that i knew nothing about. He called me by a nickname that I hardly remembered. After the first page, I closed my eyes and tried to see his face, but I could recall only the washed out gaze of the old man among the mannequins. It was probably in that moment that I became totally aware of the change. Fifteen years ago I hadn't had a house, or a car, or a garden, or a wife, or antiques. (Yes, she was a collector. A Red Cross official can get access to every home, into every old man's attic or cellar.) My friend knew nothing about my wife or the unborn child, nor about my gardening, nor about the quarrels with my neighbour who kept sprinkling the grass at wrong times and throwing his cut branches over my hedge. Nor about the fears that I was becoming an alcoholic, or about the bald spot spreading on the top of my head, or about the dark naevus on my arm. He knew someone else, someone even I had forgotten in the meantime: a boy who had once thrown a dustbin into a shop-window, a youth who had, spending summer holidays in the very same resort the letter was now mentioning, fleeced the tourists, playing quickdraw chess with them.

Was I still thinking about this while reading my wife's short message that she wasn't going to come back? Certainly: it was precisely in that moment that I felt, for the second time, the change. "We all change," I said. "The letters don't seem to connect. As if I wasn't living in one piece at all." I looked at my hands: their backs were overlayed by wrinkled skin. No, not wrinkled, just criss-crossed with tiny canals between the pores. Through the bluish, bulging veins underneath the blood was flowing. I turned my wrists over and saw the veins there too, only softer, more delicate, and the skin itself was white and smooth. The date on my watch reminded me of time again, I unclasped it and put it in my apron pocket. "My wife has left me for good on the thirteenth of April, 1986," I said. "The thirteenth of April, and I am still thirty-four. Strange." I made a few steps over the lawn. The breeze came up, the trees whispered. From the belfry a sunny windowpane flashed into my pupil. The excited, moistened earth smelled stronger. My neighbour was now trimming the ivy on his garage wall. One couldn't say that life wasn't going on. On the contrary, it was springtime, it was the beautiful time just before twilight. Not wanting to do anything reckless, I took a shovel and went behind the corner to the pile of stable manure. The previous evening, when a farmer had left it in front of the gate it was too dark to transport it to the garden beds. I began to load it into the wheelbarrow.

Then I suddenly became aware of the darkness all around me. Was it possible? Could I have been so lost in my thoughts? Had I pondered so long? But about what? What kind of thoughts? What had I been doing for hours in my garden, in the middle of the sleeping suburb? Over the pink gleam of the downtown sky the belfry stood dark, mute and upright. I began to feel the coarse weight of the shovel. I fumbled for my watch, took it from under the shears in my apron, brought it in front of my eyes. I couldn't decipher the digits. The trees were still whispering. "But what on earth are they whispering, bowing and bending like that?" I felt a softness under my feet, the soles of my boots were now so sensitive, I reached down, scooped with my hand and brought to my lips a clod of fresh, moist earth. It smelled of cypresses. I knew that my wife wasn't at home. I stood motionless, keeping my back to the house. From time to time, the chain of the neighbour's dog rattled. Bats swooped through the air. I could hear their wings flapping. And the frantic buzz of night moths. The snapping of beaks or jaws. My fingers were growing stiff, still clutching the clod. The belfry clock struck ten. There was a thin whistle inside my ear–drum. The earth was trying to tell me something. "There's no other way," I said at last. "I don't know what I am, but I know that I'm not what I used to be." It was as if I were made of obsidian, as if I were hollow, as if I were coming from elsewhere. Did the one that had lived in my body before, breaking window panes and playing chess, still find enough strength to warn me, to recall me, to recall himself? The garden around me was so strange, the houses around were so strange. Somewhere below, ants were sleeping, larvae were living their lives, a mole stirred, and miles and miles of sky overhead... Plants were reaching out with their leaves, clinging to earth with roots. Everything was alive. Among this silent, invisible budding and shifting I knew for sure: an unknown creature had assumed my appearance and taken my place in the world, my position at work, the warmth of my body, the rustle of dry leaves under my soles, the sting of snowflakes on my skin, my view of the belfry, the sound of it's bell, everything, everything. Was this the reason why I cultivated plants – because it was only a plant that had remained after me? I sensed, in darkness, nebulae, mists of shapes, webs of creepers, jointed bamboo stalks, a jungle moving in. The vegetation was primeval, it was the beginning; and now, at the end, all these irises, columbines, resedas, zinnias, lilacs, vines, peonies surrendered to the thoughtful love of the gardener, sucking him dry! Feeding on him! And I? The former I who evidently was still lingering on, or otherwise I wouldn't be standing now as if I had become lignified, as if my feet were rooted – what was he to do in presence of such impossible thoughts? Should he go to the police and try to make them believe that he had become a vegetable? Should he sit in the dark kitchen and wait for my wife, knowing she will never come back?

My thoughts were springing up like mushrooms, shrubby and mouse–grey and villous.

When I had uprooted, trampled or broken all the bushes, all the flowers; when I had torn off the boughs of the cherry and beech trees; I finally paused in the flickers of the bonfire I had made out of twigs and branches and beanpoles and tool–handles. The smell of burning meat permeated my nostrils, but it wasn't coming from my fire. I heard spurts of distant laughter. "There must be a late garden party somewhere around," I told myself, imagining I could discern my wife's excited voice above the crackling and hissing of the smoldering vegetation. "Oeopath." He couldn't hear me, whoever he was. Nobody heard me. The neighbour's house was dark. I heard the soft whirr of an unknown creature. "Something terrible has happened," I said, and drew the shear–blade across my wrists, cutting the skin under which the blue veins ran. At least the blood seemed to be real and alive. Beside me was a pile of manure, faintly outlined against the wall. I lay down on it. The manure was warm as if someone had been lying on it only a moment before. Whose mound was this? Mine? Or my wife's who had left forever? I felt the warmth less and less, the cold settling into me and replacing the blood. At last, when I began to shiver, I felt capillaries sprouting from me as root–hairs, desperately digging into the thickness of the earth.

It seemed a very long time before they let me out. Actually only seven months went by. During that time the plants often revealed themselves to me. Their rustling kept me awake during summer nights, and in the autumn, I used to find their indecipherable cracked leaves under the window sill. A rose caught fire in a vase on my bedside table. A dandelion blow–ball looked at me from between the cobblestones of the inner yard. Often I felt the urge to answer, but I neither spoke up, nor laughed, nor cried. One day in November, when my wife quietly sat at the head of my bed, watching my silence, I stumbled upon a queer thought. "I wouldn't have cut my wrists had not a residue within me still believed in Red Cross," I nearly uttered aloud, surprised not so much by this idea which was just as circumstantial and crazy as everything that crossed my mind during those months, as by the fact that it had managed to make everything so innocent and logical and even joyful. Still mute, I stretched out my hand, grasped my wife's hand, and placed its cup on my shaved head. Its touch was cool and sustained, charging me with a feeling of rising water, and I became aware that I wasn't silent any more. The water had risen up to my eyes and I sat up and cried aloud and she caressed me.

I'm sitting at this makeshift table, covered with a wine-sprinkled tablecloth, ove the round, chocolate)brown knees. The letters were large, so he could easily follow the text written in simple English. The task was almost too simple. But he had just come from lunch, warm matter, mixed with fried Kentucky chicken, was lazily and happily flowing through his body. He abandoned himself to the large letters and the rocking train rushing into the black underground.

He suddenly felt excited and wide awake. The text resting on top of the naked chocolate knees, nicely cooled in the sdesirable, of course, to understand, to grasp the meaning, but I think it's the feeling of things that is more important. My wife is in the kitchen, banging the dishes. We are going to adopt a child. My bathing trunks cut across my waist, I grew quite fat from all the medication. Well, there is another aftermath of my treatment that I can be more pleased with. I don't know how, whether from drugs or from the shocks or from the sheer act of having had my skull shaved, but somehow my hair started to grow over the bald spot. It's soft and fluffy. I know it makes my story soppy, but I can't help it. I myself have became soppy. Oeopathy, that's what I've decided to call this outpouring of sentiment. I like to imagine this man, the oeopath, sitting in his dark basement room and deciphering, with fingertips, the shuddering sobs of his patients. And that's all there is to it.

I see the children of my new neighbour. Brown, dark-eyed and skinny, they peep from behind a tree in the olive grove. Perhaps they sense in me a strangeness similar to theirs. Shall I ever write anything else? Is there something else yet to happen? I don't indulge in gardening any more, but still a tree occasionally prompts me, the murmur of the rain on leaves still implores or demands. And a twig shudders, an olive drops, a grasshopper jumps, the light skips from under the silvery leaves. Still the inhuman earth calls me: I get up and make a few steps over its trampled, cracked surface, sun–baked almost into bricks. The ground under my bare feet is so hot and so still and my wife comes now from the house and we embrace each other so that I gaze over her hair at the bay and beyond the cape towards the next one and so on, over bays and capes, all the way to the horizon, and she strokes me and tells me that everything is all right, while I stare past the zero point of the horizon, sensing the earth's roundness until tears blur my vision.

MOUSEDAY

As we are on our way to gather chestnuts, the day doesn't seem to be unusual at all. It's Sunday morning. The cold is delicate, interwoven with fresh and translucent light that thickens amidst the trees into slating sheaves, mingling edgelessly with rotting leaves underfoot. The children are nice, vivid, rosy. We are holding polythene bags in our hands. We are garbed into autumnal colours, brown, red, ochre. The girl has a muted red overcoat, her golden hair spills over the collar and down her back as she moves felinely, stepping over the roots, never stumbling, although her gaze is lifted towards me and beyond, to the thinned tree- crowns, searching for the elongated chestnut leaves.

"Wait," I say, "those are beeches, we won't find anything here, except perhaps a mushroom of some kind, though it is already late for mushrooms."

"I hope they haven't picked them all," she sighs. The little boy is too young to be in complete command of his body in the condensed, rugged space of forest hollows and shades. I am holding him by the hand and he returns the pressure, then breaks free, taking a few independent steps towards a toadstool with its red cap strewn with white dots.

"Careful, that's a fly agaric, don't touch it, that's a poisonous one."

He comes to a halt in his chequered coat.

"Fly agaric," he repeats, "fly agaric, fly agaric," memorizing almost inaudibly.

"What will happen if I touch it?"

"You'll drop dead," says the girl.

"No, but you'd be sick."

"You'd change into a toad. Or into a fly."

The boy crouches over the fly agaric, gazing at it, enchanted.

"Nice."

He cannot tear himself away, although I urge him that we must carry on, deeper into the forest to where the chestnuts grow; he withdraws his hand, stamping stubbornly until a man in blue track–suit appears on the path below us, running uphill with a dog at his heels.

"What's he doing?"

The blue track–suit keeps flashing from among the trees, becoming ever smaller.

"The dog is chasing him."

"No, he's taking it for a walk."

"He's jogging. They all do it nowadays. Run, that is."

"Someone's after him."

"Who?"

"He's just fat and wants to slim."

"He isn't that fat. He isn't nearly as fat as you are, daddy."

"Who's after him?"

First the rustling dies away, then the thud of his strides over the trampled ground and we are alone again. I gaze around, everywhere the trees rise up, it is quiet, veiling walls of the morning are stepping asunder, the ferns tremble in the sunny specks, we are quite alone, the children and I, the somnolent forest and sky all around us.

"Let's go! Move!"

"Where to?"

"To where chestnuts are, of course, over there across the hill, they certainly grow there, we must just reach the dell, we'll fill our bags there and then we'll go home, cut the chestnuts, bake them and eat them up."

"I'll keep mine."

"You can't keep them. They'd go mouldy."

But the boy is, as usually, skipping his tiny thoughts too fast for me. "Are there any wolves here?"

I smile.

"No, there aren't any wolves in these forests any more, there are no more wolves, they died out, the hunters have killed them all."

"With guns?"

I nod and walk on. The boy tires in the middle of the slope, his legs giving way. For a while he resists gravity, then he slumps. I take hold of him under the arms, lifting him piggyback with one movement, and he settles astride my neck allowing me to clasp my fingers around his ankles. Surely he's looking about inquisitively as I walk up the hill, he's so high and he's the first to see the engrossed pair at the bench where the footpaths diverge. Nevertheless he is quiet until we have left the embraced pair far above and started to descent into a gorge overgrown with chestnuts.

"Do they love each other?"

"Uh–uh."

"Like you and mummy?"

"They have only just begun."

"Begun what?"

"To love each other."

"Is that good?"

"Good, why not, everything that has just begun is good," I answer, hearing the bells from behind the hill, summoning to mass. The children hear them too, we stop, listening for some time to the even, melodious ringing.

"It's the church–bells," says the girl.

"They are tolling."

"They are calling the people into the church."

"Tolling–calling? Tolling–calling."

"Daddy, what exactly is a church?"

"A place of worship."

"Of what?"

"Where people talk to their God."

"Daddy, tell me, but this time be serious, all right? – is there really a god?"

"Hm, sometimes there is, sometimes there isn't, I mean, for some there is, for others there isn't."

"How come?"

I shrug.

"Isn't there one for you?"

"Listen, some people believe in him and for them he exists, others believe there isn't and for them he doesn't. As for myself, I don't think there is one, either."

"Uh–uh," says the girl, moving, plunging downwards.

"Chestnuuuuts!" she calls out.

"Chest–nuts, chest–nuts," the boy keeps singing in two tones, echoing the bells, expanding his chant with another new word, "Chest–nuts exist, chest–nuts exist!" He begins to twist on my shoulders, he wants to get down. I reach back with my hands, touch his body, take hold of him and swing him over my head to the ground.

Strollers rarely come across this damp and sombre dell. There's plenty of chestnuts, the fruit making a blanket beneath the trees, even more of them hidden below the layer of mouldering leaves and tiny twigs left from the last winter. At first we gather the ones that have fallen out of their husks by themselves, then we get some sticks and start picking out the prickly shells from the layers of withered nature. The children are bringing them to me, afraid of the spines, I am smashing the husks with my heel, parting them with stiff fingers, so that the chestnuts can roll out, and the children pack them into their bags, sometimes quarrelling as to which is whose, who saw it first, who brought it to me. In the meantime, the sun rises up, the ground steams, I open ever new husks automatically, reflecting upon how much more shall I have to tell them yet, how little they know about life. I hear the girl's muted outcry, I look at her as she crouches amongst the leaves, parting them once again: the hardened soil has opened up, disclosing underneath the bleached skeleton of some tiny animal, a mouse or a shrew or a mole.

"Oh no! What is it?"

"Probably a mouse."

"Is it dead?"

"It is and it isn't, a mouse isn't aware of its death, death is something you have to be aware of, and a mouse cannot die because it has no consciousness, it's immortal, in a way."

The children have already become used to my philosophizing and they accept it with a cautious, absent–minded silence. They may be right. Even I wonder, this melting morning, about my Pythian answers.

The boy touches the tiny bones, his thumb and forefinger caressing the frail skull, excited he fingers it over and over, he has to touch everything, a little while ago it was the toadstool, now it's the mouse.

"Perhaps it's not a mouse at all," says the girl.

"Yes, it could be a shrew."

"I didn't mean that."

"Well, what did you mean?"

She shrugs.

"Perhaps it's not a mouse... or a shrew... perhaps it's something else. Something quite different."

She doesn't want to tell me.

The boy is still touching the bones that are too slender to be lifted.

53

"Will I be a mouse now?"

"No."

"I'll be a mouse."

"No, you can't be a mouse."

"Why not?"

"Oh, shut up!"

We are silent for a while. Hesitatingly the boy removes his hand. We cover the skeleton with clods of thawed soil and leaves.

"Well, if we want to fill our bags," I say, feeling their indecision, "we'd better hurry."

It gets colder and darker when we scrabble silently on, filling our bags, slowly working our way up the slope of the next ridge over which the wind is now carrying the solitary chime from the churchyard. All of a sudden the bags are nearly full and we come to a halt not quite knowing what to do next.

"Are the people going into the church again?"

"No, that's the death–bell, someone's dead, they are going to the funeral."

The boy stares intently through the trees below, towards the marshy plain, trying to hide his numb hands into his pockets.

"The mouse? Is it the mouse?"

"Is it ringing because we buried the mouse?"

"Daddy, we can go now back and you can revive the mouse."

The uneasiness strikes me then for the second time: I hear the stifled breathing of the forest, the sky is leaning upon the hills beyond the moor, it clings to the earth, not wanting to let go, everything is motionless and even I am fettered in this embrace. I shift from one foot to the other to tear myself out of it.

"You know it can't be done," I say, waving a hand, "that's silly, did we come to gather chestnuts or are we just going to stand here doing goodness knows what?"

Did they expect exactly those words? It seems so: they don't pay attention to me at all. It is as if they were reading from the same book, but constantly jumping ahead of me, to the next page. The boy suddenly discovers he's hungry and says he wants to go home, the girl says she'll be late for her badminton. I gaze at the sun suspended in the south, small and pale, surrounded by tattered clouds, it is close to midday, I march after the children who are going back along our trail, we halt at the bottom of the dell by the heaps of leaves and emptied, squashed husks, we are quite small among the thick trunks, the children stirring the leaves, no longer remembering where we buried the skeleton.

"Do you think he's gone?"

"Who?"

"The mouse."

Taken aback, I realize I don't understand. Was my mind equally strange when I was a child?

"Let's go, let's go," I say, taking them by the hand. The ravine is as lonesome and sombre as some actual ancient burial ground, and up the slope my heart begins to pound while the children are for a wonder sturdy and agile, overtaking my every step so that it seems as if it was them who were helping me, guiding me out of the forest.

They have stopped asking me about the mouse, but I am too tired to wonder any more. Out of breath, I reach the top. In spite of my dizziness I set the boy piggyback, hurrying past the bench, trying with a song to divert the children, to draw them away from the pair who are now sitting apart, the girl with red–rimmed eyes, twisting the handkerchief in the cup of her hands, the man staring ahead, his face tight. I urge my daughter to walk faster. I decide that we won't go over the hill where some new trap is possibly waiting for us under the leaves. Instead, I turn down the forest path, walking quickly, the weight of the boy bouncing around on my shoulders. When I round a mossy boulder, I catch sight of the man in the blue track–suit holding a leash with an open collar. He is gazing around him, jerkily turning his head.

"Has the dog run away from him?"

"Has the man run away from the dog?"

Of course, he is looking for his dog. Why not? The dog must be somewhere around here, following its hunting instinct or sniffing at some other dog's traces. Or maybe it ran off to fetch his master a stick. Or a branch.

A leash? A branch?

And I can't help it any more, my mind has wandered to far. The skin at the nape of my neck contracts and hardens, and an image forms on it, made of needles and pins. I recognize it without seeing it, creeping up from behind me: the branch, the leash, the swaying body.

I rub my neck, tearing the vision off, and look at the children. They are watching me intently.

Without any warning, I grab them and pull them, forcing them to run.

As we hurry off, the girl falls silent. She is pondering, I can feel it.

The boy still wonders.

"Daddy, perhaps the dog was a wolf?"

And, after a second, "Daddy, are there any witches here?"

"No, the dog wasn't a wolf. No, there aren't any witches here," I reply curtly, at the same time imagining the end of our trip: how my doubts about paternal powers gradually increase until the two already grown-up children, actually my daddy and mummy, carry me home and put me to bed. It is obvious that the whole world is at their disposal while I have retained only the closing space of denial, the passive role of a disbeliever, forced to set bounds to their lives. But what is supposed to happen on a day like this when their world invades mine so that all my strongholds give way? Through breathlessness and perspiration, shudders begin to pervade me, numbly I set one foot in front of the other, one in front of the other, letting the children pull me, push me. The forest is too autumnal, too dark. The first drops are falling. The children, like some resolute Hansel and Gretel, keep leading me towards rescue, I'm running between them, stumbling over twisted roots. The drops are very cold, colder even than the air in my lungs. The reports I hear, booming like distant rifle shots, are very sinister until the girl says, "The soldiers, must they train shooting even on Sundays?" and I remember, yes, of course, there is a shooting- range right over the hill.

"Just like your badminton," I gasp.

"Are they dangerous?" asks the boy.

"No, no! There is a slope in between, the bullets couldn't reach us, the shooting-range is fenced-in, and anyway, they are using blanks," I keep panting, but nevertheless I race, bent forward, thinking only that I mustn't trip over, not just now, for I don't want the children to pick me up and heave and carry me out of the forest. Do they sense any of this, or do they think we are running from the rain? They are silent again, this race is an effort to them too, and something mute, so it seems, is going on among us, within us, something that can never end.

But the end is nearly there. In the next moment we are at the road that rims the forest along the railway, separating it from the town, full of houses and wires, cars and windows, the tension lessens, it is only a few hundred paces more to go along the deserted Sunday pavements, and before I know our house rises in front of us at the end of the street. Then the bell tolls again, from the cathedral spire, it is one o'clock, the sound stirring up memories.

"Daddy,« says the girl, "but there was one before, wasn't there?"

"One what?"

"God."

"Before? What do you mean?"

"Before he went to pick chestnuts," says the boy enigmatically.

"No, silly, before, in olden times."

"Well, everybody believed in him, so he must have been right there among them," I say, gazing after a vanishing car full of Sunday passengers.

"Perhaps he died?"

"Died?"

"Yes, he doesn't live any more because he died. He couldn't just vanish into thin air."

"No, no, there is no god, and besides, god is something that cannot die, something eternal."

The girl desists. But god, despite my words, doesn't leave me, and while we are entering and my wife is divesting us of our clothes, putting them to dry by the fire, I imagine him how he has dragged himself into solitude, how he is awaiting death while the

57

table is already set for lunch and the children shake the
chestnuts out of bags and onto the floor and set them into rows,
as soldiers or toy cars, and I start shouting at them to stop it at
once and take their seats at the table, just like a very dying god in
whom, of the whole world, only two children still believe –
because they believe in everything.

And yet one must live, one must live as long as possible, with
this thought, the last before lunch, before I silently start breaking
our bread, I stare through the window towards the forest
overgrowing the nearest hill. At the back of this hill there lies
another one. Beyond is the dell in which, under mouldering,
decomposing leaves, in the loosened earth, amidst the grubs and
larvae and the rotting, decaying seeds and twigs and fruits lies
the skeleton of the immortal, everlasting god–mouse.

LIFE STORY

S tepping out of his car, Satler immediately felt the unpleasant, half prickling and half stabbing sensation inside his nostrils: the moist inner hairs were freezing. Here it was even colder than downtown. In such cold, one would expect the air to be crisp, but it was pasty and it resisted being stirred. Forcing it into his lungs, Satler took an imprudently deep breath and the air, it seemed, immediately froze onto the tissue of his lungs. As if he had swallowed a glass of crumbled ice. He coughed it out and then in pain forced himself to breathe shallowly, with bronchial tubes only. He turned up the collar of his overcoat and made a few tentative steps over the ice–covered snow on the lawn in front of the building.

The body was lying in the middle of the asphalt pavement, covered with a sheet. Before hitting the ground, it must have screamed out or maybe the people had been waken up by the crash itself: through the moonlight, Satler could make out the dark silhouettes peering from among the ice–ferns on the shut window–panes.

There were no traces of blood. The dark specks on the sheet were the shadows, interspersed between the moonlit craters of the creased, frosted linen. "Morning," said Satler and the two patrolmen who had been stamping the ground, trying to keep their feet warm, froze into attention. Now they looked like a guard of honour, with the covered body in between.

"Good morning, sir. Want to take a closer look?"

Satler glanced at his wrist–watch. It was a quarter past four. "When did it happen?"

"At half past three."

Satler drew off the frozen sheet. For some reason, the body underneath seemed to be feathery, even fluffy, as if it had lost all weight during its fall. This strange impression was probably due to the fact that no bone had been left uncrushed within the frail, juvenile body. Satler shook the notion away. Four o'clock in the morning was the time of low blood sugar, of insomnia, of dreamy apparitions – and of suicides.

The body was lying on its belly, the left leg twisted and thrown over the back, its sole almost touching the nape. The other leg was hidden somewhere beneath the body. There were no visible lacerations, no bones protruding from under the skin. The blood, if any, was underneath. "Where's the pathologist?"

One of them shrugged, "We called forensics immediately. Due to be here any moment now."

Satler was silently watching the body. The fact that it was clad in pyjamas added to its vulnerability, if that was the appropriate expression to be used in the case of a dead man. Its stripes seemed to be painted, added as an afterthought. Satler bent over the body. The bare foot was white, as if covered with rime. It was the uncallosed foot of a young man, a youth. The toenails were neat, well–shaped, tender as fingernails. Satler seized the toes, at first gently, than firmly, trying to flex them. They were icy and seemed to slightly resist the pressure.

"Are you positive about the time of death?"

"People heard him fall. Somebody phoned immediately afterwards. That was at three thirty–five."

Satler crouched lower. The face clung to the ground, hidden between the left arm and the hump of the right shoulder. He wanted to feel the jaw, but it wasn't possible without turning the head around. Of all the face, only the left eye could be touched. Sliding the eyelid with the tip of his forefinger, Satler closed it and opened it again. It wasn't rigid. The eye, very dark in the gloom, stared knowingly ahead. The pupil wasn't dilated but the iris seemed enormous, deep and alive. It wasn't the first time that Satler had seen such a look. What unnerved him was the flashback, triggered by it, a scene from a movie, probably some

60

TV documentary: there were people in it, clad in similar striped pajamas with nothing underneath, nothing but frail bones under taut white skin. They were alive but they stared towards the camera out of the hollows of their knowing eyes. Satler stood up.

"Just checking the flexibility of the eyelids," he said, feeling the superfluity of his words. The patrolmen knew perfectly well what he was doing. One of them said: "I thought so. Any signs of rigor mortis?" Satler detected a hint of uneasiness behind the question.

"You see, it is much too early for any signs – if he was alive when he fell. It's just a hunch, but the body seems to be too cold," he explained.

"It's very cold," said the patrolman. "The weather I mean. Below zero, I believe."

"Yes, yes," he said, "Sure, yes." And after a pause, "Did you carry out the identification?"

"He's a tenant. Pelhan is up there in his flat."

"Pelhan, Pelhan...?"

"Sergeant Pelhan, sir."

"Aha. What floor?"

"The eleventh."

"And the name?"

They didn't know.

The eleventh floor: approximately twenty–five yards. That could well explain the absence of visible lacerations. Falling from such a height, the body driven by enormous acceleration doesn't have time to burst; it collapses like a black hole.

There was a darkish smear on the cadaver's left wrist. Not quite knowing what was he hoping to find, maybe a wrist–cut or an injection oedema, something to base his hunch on, Satler nearly kneeled onto the ice and half–turned the wrist. It was a blue tattoo, a serpent or maybe a vine leaf, entwining an anchor. Peering closely, he rolled back the sleeve that had covered the top of the anchor. There was an inscription, made of abbreviations: ADAI. Or was it a word? A name? The eye was dark, it could be Jewish...

"Who called? His family?"

"I'm afraid the man didn't identify himself."

"Yes, yes."

There was something wrong.

Standing up, Satler raised his eyes. The moonlight coloured the building with a bluish, fluorescent gleam. Some of the windows were alight and Satler could easily count up to the eleventh floor. All the windows were dark.

In uneasy silence he could hear the chattering teeth of the other patrolman. He lowered his gaze. The patrolman's face had a bluish colour of moonlight. It wore the expression of rigid concentration but the lower jaw was trembling. Satler drew the sheet over the body and thrust his stiff fingers into the coat-pocket.

"Okay, I got the point. We can't wait any longer in this cold. The pathologist probably can't get his car started. Call him and tell him to wait. Send for an ambulance. Remove the body to his lab and tell him I want an immediate postmortem. The main question is the abnormally low body temperature, irrespective of the cold. I want him also to examine his stomach contents and take a blood sample. With special regard to traces of intoxication or drug-poisoning. I'll be waiting for the report up there."

With obvious relief, the older of the patrolmen trod off towards their car. While Satler crossed the few steps over the strip of barren asphalt to the door, he heard desperate, scuffling sounds. He didn't turn his head, but in the door-pane he saw the reflection of the patrolman who had been left behind, awkwardly stamping the ground around the gleaming mound and beating his chest and flanks with wing-like movements of his arms.

The air inside smelled of stale cabbage or unemptied garbage bins, but at least it was warm. With the relief of uninhibited breathing, there came also a sudden wave of exhaustion. While waiting for the elevator to come down, he had to lean against the wall, still catching his breath. Gradually, the constriction inside his lungs subsided, and when he stepped into the cage and closed his eyes, only tiredness remained. He had been on duty for fourteen hours without a break. This was probably the only reason of his premonitions. Or maybe not? Really, why had he felt from the very beginning that this wasn't an ordinary suicide?

The pyjamas, yes. In almost twenty years of his service he had rarely seen a suicide improperly dressed. Funny people. Always tidying things up. Writing letters, beseeching, accusing; settling accounts, paying off their petty debts, cleaning their apartments, caring about their appearance. Surely, they were doing it in the middle of the night, but usually dressed up, even clean shaven. They didn't really believe, not with their whole being, that they were going to die. Dissociative amnesia. That's why they were making appointments for the next day: one part of their consciousness couldn't accept what was going to happen. Satler remembered the words from a course in forensic psychiatry: even while falling, a suicide still secretly believes that he is going to collect his pieces down there, put them together into a better shape and start anew.

Yes, but the amnestic touch could just as well explain the pyjamas away. Someone unaware of his secret intention would easily go to bed and even sleep till the moment of crisis...

There were two corridors in the eleventh floor, with many doors. Satler took a few steps into the northern one and closed his eyes. When he heard the click of the light going off, he opened them and started slowly to turn his head. After some time, a thin crack of light far away came into the centre of his focus. He thought he could discern faint voices. With outstretched arms, he made for them and almost immediately bumped into the door. He had misjudged the distance.

When Pelhan opened, Satler swayed dizzily in the warmth flowing out of the heated apartment. He tried to decipher the name on the door–plate but the light was too dazzling. Pelhan led him into the dinette on the right of the narrow anteroom. The voices had been coming from there. An old couple, well, not old, but bent and frail in their dismay, stood up not knowing what to do. Pelhan introduced Satler. The woman was obviously too upset to react. The old man sat her down onto her stool and then went to make some more tea for Satler. It was out of the question that they'd had anything to do with the tragic incident. The old man suddenly asked him his name and Pelhan introduced him for the second time. It was only now that Satler caught the name: Bordon. Definitely gentile. The black eyes were probably of Italian or French origin.

The couple were still in a state of shock, thinking of Satler not as a policeman but as Pelhan's friend or maybe a neighbour.

63

Satler wondered whether he should offer some words of sympathy but decided against it. There was a curious moment when they were all sitting at the table and talking about the cold. But even that wasn't as unusual as it seemed. Satler had experienced similar moments before. He didn't mind if people acted funnily – he was more inclined to become suspicious when they tried to control their responses.

"Excuse me, just for a second, if you don't mind," he said at last and beckoned to Pelhan into the anteroom.

"So what's going on?"

"I beg your pardon, sir?"

"Well, what do we have here, an accident or a suicide? What do the parents say?"

Pelhan was startled. "An accident? What makes you say so? Because that is exactly what they maintain. But it could hardly have been an accident; there are safety windows in this building, opening with the upper part inwards. He had to stand on the sill and squeeze himself through the side opening which is narrow even at the upper half. I mean, he actually had to climb way up the window in order to get through the crevice."

"I see. But such a window is quite as inconvenient as far as a suicide is concerned. There's definitely something funny about it... Did you check his record?"«

"No, not yet. I mean, the parents..."

"Never mind the parents, just check the record. I'll have a word with them."

Satler went back into the dinette where he found a cup of oversugared tea waiting for him. In their confusion, the couple had probably sweetened it twice. At least it was hot. Satler could sip it only slowly, cooled with air, so sore had his throat become outside. Hearing Pelhan's muffled voice from behind the door he said: "Look, I know it is hard... I'm sorry, but I have to ask you a few questions, for the sake of the record..."

They stared at him. "The record?" said Bordon.

"Just a few questions for the sake of protocol."

"We have always loved and respected each other," the woman suddenly said and this statement, even if out of place, sounded so final that Satler decided not to probe deeper for the time being. "Could I, please, take a look at the site of the... tragic occurence?" Bordon started to rise, with a puzzled expression. "Don't bother," said Satler, "it's all right, I'll just take a quick look around."

Pelhan had just hung up. "No record whatsoever." They went to the room which was narrow like most rooms in newly-built council tenement buildings but for some reason seemed spacious. Maybe because the window was opened and the visible cold (Satler saw the vapour of his breathing) connected the room with the outside, or because of the scattered objects which had acquired, for Satler's working mind, the properties of signs and landmarks on a full-size survey map?

The room was a mess. The bed was unmade, the small table by the window was littered with paper. There was a slipper on the floor, overturned, nearly touching a chessboard with pieces launched far into the middle game. Satler crouched and studied the position. No, it wasn't a game, it was apparently a problem, mate in one. It was intriguing. Not the problem itself which wasn't too demanding, but could it be possible that this unsolved situation was some sort of a message? A farewell letter? "You didn't touch anything, did you?"

"No. However, there's nothing much to be seen."

"Where's the other slipper?"

"I beg you pardon, sir?"

"There's only one slipper here."

"Aha. Yes." Pelhan, obviously tired, tried to show some interest. "What do you make of it, sir?"

"Nothing. Better not to make guesses at this stage of investigation. All kinds of wild ideas spring up if one lets one's imagination loose. Like: he could have lost the other one during his fall. But then, why on earth would he jump with only one slipper? And if he shook off this one in the commotion, I don't know, maybe fighting or having the shakes or whatever, how come he didn't upset the chess-pieces?" Pelhan nodded, but remained silent. Satler stood up and turned around, glancing at the posters and pictures on the wall above the bed. Cherry blossoms, a mountain lake during a tempest, pop-singers with stereotyped faces and headresses, another stormy landscape,

65

cottonpickers, a Chinese painting of a snow-capped landscape, another Chinese painting of an unknown bird with silvery-green feathers. On the opposite wall there was a book-shelf with maybe eighty or ninety books. Satler went through them. Most of the authors were unfamiliar. There was also some poetry. Satler went over to the table. "This is his handwriting? Did you read it?"

"Not thoroughly. But it definitely isn't a farewell note. It seems to be some kind of a scheme for a composition."

There were at least ten sheets of paper but some of them were crumpled after only two or three words had been written. Satler quickly sorted them out. Two sheets were written all over in nearly unreadable, pointed handwriting. On some of the others there were abandoned variations of the same initial sentences that gave evidence of the author's painstaking and uncertain endeavour. Satler pulled out the drawers. They were empty, but from the unfaded ink-stains, the pencil-sharpenings, and the thumbtack holes it was evident that the drawers had been in use not long ago. Putting his nose into each drawer, Satler could smell nothing but dust, wood and a faint trace of glue. He sat on the chair and started to read.

Every story has a pattern, life doesn't have one.

Adamec slowly getting mad. (The meaning of the surname.)

The turning point: he doesn't see the story of his life. The everyday life of the others seems to be only a cover.

Every life-story is like a composition. The beginning, the middle, the end. But not his life. The moral: what one needs is his own story. Also: to fathom the others. Examples of other people's life stories. The more simple cliches the better: birth-death, rise-fall. Therefore, his life devoid of this inner structure. Random. Direct cause: it could be the army.

To be cut off from the course.

The course: the direction given by the initial circumstances (birth, parents, school). Inertia. Conclusion: inertia is life.

"Blut ist Leben." (Vampirism.)

But with no blood...

Perhaps he recognizes himself in a children's history book, depicted as a Neanderthal man.

66

Nature as a initial force.

The mammoth hunt.

The spear for the first time.

Summer.

Better early autumn. Beginnings of decay. Mother Nature.

Afternoon strolls with his wife.

Here, for the first time, I mention his son. (Very late. Dreamlike impression of real things arising as afterthoughts.)

Other people hiding something. Another life? The other life? They have their hidden lives.

What does he have? (At least his hidden madness, but he doesn't know it.)

That was the end of the first page (or was it the second?). It didn't seem to have any direct link with the author's death. Still, some words were sticking out conspicuously: ... fall... madness... absence of blood...

Satler set his mind to reread it in case he had overlooked anything but after a moment he let his hand drop down. It was like reading a modern poem: he could understand the words but the meaning of the whole eluded him. If there was any meaning at all. Adolescent fiction...

"What was his first name?"

"Peter."

"Peter Bordon..." Obviously, Pelhan was following the similar train of thoughts. "Maybe he did it because he couldn't publish."

"Hm. Unlikely at his age. How old was he? Seventeen?"

"Eighteen."

"Eighteen... Okay, let us stick to material facts. The window." He stepped onto the chair and from there onto the desk. Raising his left foot, he thrust it through the crevice between the window–rim and the in–bent pane. It was easier than he had expected. "You see, Pelhan," he said, "it's not so difficult. And mind you, I'm not so slim. With little effort, I could squeeze my thigh out, and with MY body outside, I'd have just to lean against the air and let gravity take over." But he didn't proceed. It wasn't only that he was uncomfortable, with his shin dangling out in the cold: there was another, well-known sensation spreading throughout his body. When he had been sixteen he had been foolish enough to join, for once, some fell-climbing friends. Trying to keep up with them, he got stuck in the middle of a crumbly rock-wall and he barely managed to cling there, resisting the steady pull of gravity, until they returned and helped him descend. By that evening his feeling of shame was already stronger than the afterglow of physical dread, but later on, whenever he stumbled upon this memory, remembering the tension in his clinging limbs, remembering the small blue eye of the glacial lake down below, and the silence, and the solitude, his mental fingers unclasped and he dived, tumbling and shrieking through the air.

"My God, it's cold outside," he heard himself say as he pulled the leg back into the room. "I can hardly feel my toes." Awkwardly, he stepped onto the chair and from there onto the floor. "Well, I don't think there's much else to be seen here anyway. This writing," he picked the sheets up, "it appears to be about madness. Even a 'fall' is mentioned there, but hidden beneath the meaning of failure... One of those exasperating messages that can be deciphered only after the final act, I am afraid."

They returned to the kitchen and Satler started to interrogate Bordon inobtrusively about his son. It wasn't the first time that he had to investigate a suicide with this type of history: a good-tempered, inquisitive, spontaneous child who had suddenly grown into a taciturn, reflective adolescent, too earnest, too solitary...

"Could you tell me more about his habits," said Satler, gazing attentively towards the man and at the same time aware that he wasn't really going to listen to his answers. He started to fight this sudden loss of interest, suspecting that its cause was just as inexplicable as his previous suspicions. There was something unnatural about this case, something that had attracted his attention from the very first and that was probably the very thing that was now dissuading him from pursuing the matter more thoroughly. Nevertheless he couldn't force himself to think about it. Yes, there was something in the cold, dark, messy room, something urgently seeking first to be discovered and then to be forgotten, but here, in the dinette, it was warm, bright and tidy...

Like a meadow on a sunny afternoon, with the drowsy purr of lawn-mowers down in the valley. He lay on his back, blinking at the sun, and later he strolled by the edge of the forest and found some fruit, rowanberries, or perhaps they were mushrooms, and when he had filled the basket he sat down on a tree-stump and lit a match...

It was after he had inhaled the sweet-scented smoke and after the feeling of guilt had pervaded his chest that he became aware he was dreaming. He opened his eyes. The old man was still talking about his son. His wife was gone. The dinette seemed to be even tidier now. There were napkins on the table, and a jar of honey. The kettle in the kitchen was babbling. Then the woman came from behind the partition to take the cups. As she did so, the hand of the man, who was still talking, rested on her hand, lightly, briefly, as if perching, and than took off and let her pick up his cup. The motion was transitory, barely perceptible, and yet it shook Satler out of his stupefaction as if the man's eyeless hand (for it seemed to be, in that moment, a living being) had suddenly grabbed him by the heel in the middle of the rock wall.

"Okay," said Satler, "thank you. Thank you." He glanced at his watch. Half past five. "Now, if you would just let me finish reading this..."

Darkness. Black. Insomnia. Suicidal fantasies. Insomnia. Nature, in various forms. Moving. Phases of life. Job? Unspecified. But we know he has one.

At the tailor.

When he meets Helen, he's attracted by her secret. The secret of a life story.

Her secret: She loves him. (?)

(Love giving meaning etc...)

Fits of rage. He tells his wife: I think I'm going crazy.

Rage against the child?

He meets Helen on a trip. This seems to be the beginning of a story. In order to get hold of the secret, to get involved into a story, he lets himself be drawn to her.

Their relation.

Everything developing slowly.

Nature. Strolls.

Situation even now the same.

No story possible.

Cuts off. Helena vanishes. He vanishes her.

Autumn. Winter. Time.

The news (through a mutual friend) that she gave birth.

It could be that he is the father.

Birthday party of his legal child. Big scene. The child's joy. The other one lives alone, without father, unrecognized, like Jesus, far from Herodotus' eyes.

Perhaps this is the beginning of a true story? (Aha, aha, why not? To be recognized as such, every story must repeat some previous one!)

Fantasies, fantasies. The writing, no matter how pessimistic in spirit, seemed to be completely discordant with the real situation. It was obviously a sketch of some sort, a plot–plan, but the story itself... Yes, the child as the last hope, so to say, but Peter Bordon hadn't been married and hadn't had a son... Surely, he didn't even have a girlfriend.

"What about his emotional life. Was he in love? Did he have any relationship?"

"I don't believe so," said Bordon and Satler was sure he wasn't trying to conceal anything.

"Helen," he said, "does this name mean anything to you?"

Of course, it was fictional.

Satler shrugged his shoulders. "You said he had been writing a lot. Did he get anything published?"

Bordon shook his head. "No. Everything was just like this. Or he would, for instance, devise a book, a novel, and lay out the chapters, you know, the titles, beautiful titles, beautiful mottoes, but after having written a page of two of the first chapter he would just discard it and start something new. Plans, schemes, titles, but actually he could never really finish a story, a proper story. If you ask me, he wasn't really writing, he was just day–dreaming."

"Yes, the problem of a story... Did he talk with you about this... this comparison... between the life and the story? About his... inability to make a story out of his life?"

"We never discussed his stories. He was too self–conscious about his writing. That's also the reason why you can't see more of it. He was destroying the things that he didn't like. Almost everything, that is."

Himself included, thought Satler. "What about friends? You say he didn't have any real friends. But what about... you know... school–mates, other young people with similar interests? People with whom he would have liked to discuss things like literature, life...?"

"I wish he had somebody," said Bordon. "But he was quite lonesome for the last two or three years. Not that we wouldn't let him. Come on, go out, have fun, enjoy yourself, I kept telling him. But he preferred staying at home, reading, writing, learning..." Bordon started to cry.

"He was really such a nice boy," said the woman in a normal voice but wringing her fluttering hands. Satler felt a surge of embarrassment. He knew that the couple had already started unconsciously to reproach themselves, but what on earth could he say?

At that moment the phone rang and Satler gladly retreated into the anteroom. It was the forensic laboratory; so far, they had found no signs of intoxication or struggle. Considering the exceptionally cold weather, the surface temperature of the body wasn't lower than could be expected, and the rectal temperature was confirming the time of death as somewhere around 3 AM.

"That's it," said Satler to Pelhan after he had hung up. "It's nearly six o'clock. I've had enough of this. I'm going straight home. You can go through the paper–work, all right? Let's say good–bye to the parents."

They returned to the dinette. The couple seemed to had regained some of their previous, albeit feinted composure. The woman offered them a drink before leaving. Satler thanked them, cleared his throat and at last managed to express his condolence. Bordon listened carefully. Then he started to rise from behind the table. "Don't, don't, no need to," babbled Satler with a sudden premonition that Bordon was going to tell him something that wouldn't be related to the investigation but that would intimately bind him with the family. Like showing him a family photo album and telling him about his son's childhood. "We'll find our way out. Thanks for tea and everything. If there's anything we could do, just give us a ring..." But Bordon, when he had got up, just thanked him solemnly and showed him out, clicking the corridor lights on.

Outside, only a marker–flag stuck into frozen ground showed where the body had been lying. With the moonlight gone, it was still darker than before but some of the neighbouring windows were lit up. People were dressing, getting ready for their early shifts.

Both the keyholes in the car doors were frozen. Luckily, Pelhan had a lighter. Then they had to scrape the ice from the windscreen. Satler had hardly managed to start the engine when the frostwork began to form on the outer side of the windscreen and they had to stop and scrub it off repeatedly. At the beginning, when it was still cold inside, they couldn't talk, trying to stop the chattering of their teeth. Later, with warmth, there came the stupor. They were silent all the way downtown, too tired and too sleepy to say anything but good–bye to each other at the end of the journey.

Alone, Satler drove home still thinking about Bordon. He carefully went over all the evidence. By the time he pulled into his garage he knew he could dismiss the case once and for all. His premonitions had been ill–founded and arbitrary. Of course, the exact reasons for the suicide were still largely obscure, but it could at least be inferred from the evidence that Peter Bordon, this over–sensitive and inhibited youngster, hadn't been induced or driven to commit suicide by any other person. Besides, his relative isolation and self–restraint were a reasonable guarantee that his suicide, contagious as suicides were, wouldn't spread further around. The primary aim of a suicide investigation was to establish the facts considering the possibility of recurrence. In the case of Peter Bordon no preventive measures seemed necessary and the case should be therefore dismissed.

The elevator was out of order and he had to go up to the sixth floor on foot, tiredly ascending through the early morning scents of ham–and–eggs, peeled oranges and milk that had boiled over. After the chattering and murmuring of kettles and people in other apartments, the silence in his own made him uneasy. He went to the kitchen: the table was empty except for the ash-tray full of cigarette butts. The smell of stale tobacco mixed with the sweetish odour of the leftovers by the sink. He sat down and watched the cigarette butts, fighting the sudden desire to smoke. One of the butts was quite long. Actually the cigarette was almost untouched: the smoker had lighted the filter instead of the tip and immediately discarded it.

Finally, the urge was too strong and he stood up and went into the bedroom. Marika's foot with glossy toe-nails was protruding from under the cover. For some reason, Satler couldn't stand this sight and he pulled the blanket over it. The blanket was heaving noiselessly.

Than he shook the shoulder beneath it.

"Mmm?"

"Wake up," he said.

"Mhmm." She wrapped the blanket over her head.

He went into the kitchen and put on the coffee-pot. He emptied the ash-tray and took his shoes off. Then he poured the boiling water over the instant coffee and again felt like smoking.

Saturday. He must rest now but they could go somewhere in the afternoon.

At last he heard Marika getting out of bed.

"When did you come in?"

"Nearly an hour ago."

She glanced at the oven clock. "Why must you always make things up? You hardly had time enough to take your shoes off. Or to make coffee. By the way, did you make me one?"

"No. You were asleep, weren't you?"

"Asleep... I think I'm entitled at least to sleep. And I was awake till past four, waiting for Boris."

"Boris? Where did he go?"

"I don't know where he went. It was Friday night, so I suppose he went to some party. And he didn't come back, at least I didn't hear him staggering about." Scratching her neck, she poured the water into the cup.

"Listen," he said, "what's going on? What's happening to your son? Don't you realize he's only fifteen?"

"He's your son just as well. And you are supposed to know everything better than me. After all, you are an investigator, aren't you?"

He didn't say anything.

She raised her cup.

"Your ulcer still giving you pains?" he asked.

"Yes. Am I too edgy for you?"

"No. But I don't know why you drink coffee then," he said.

"Who's telling me!"

"There were eighteen cigarette butts in the ash-tray."

"I was worried about Boris."

He finished his coffee and carried the cup to the sink. "It's freezing like hell outside!"

"Oh hell, and I have to go to the market. Would you be a dear and go instead of me, while you still have your clothes on?"

"No chance! My feet are still numb. I'm going to bed. I've been working for sixteen hours! And anyway, you are never satisfied with things I bring home from the market. No thanks!"

"I wasn't sleeping either."

"Yes, you can say that again. Otherwise you couldn't have smoked all those cigarettes."

They fell silent. Marika was sipping coffee. With satisfaction, he realized she didn't dare to light a cigarette.

The dawn was seeping through the window-panes.

"So you are not going?" she said.

He stood up and went to Boris' room. The bed was empty, untouched. He went over to the bedside table and pulled out the drawer. There was nothing in it but old coins of every kind. He paddled with his fingers through this copper and nickle and silver sea, in vain trying to reach the bottom. Still, it seemed to him that the level had lowered. If the boy would at least keep collecting them and not steal from himself.

74

Then he smelled the cigarette smoke and went back to the kitchen.

She was looking past him.

"You do that," he said. "Go on."

"Don't you understand that it regulates my digestion? I have all kinds of troubles with my duodenum and I don't need constipation as well." But when he moved over she nearly recoiled. He stopped short. "You're nervous..."

"You mean you are nervous."

"I am not nervous, it's just that I didn't sleep and that I'm trying to get rid of my smoking habit and I already told you I would knock the cigarette out of your mouth or start smoking again if you were going to go on smoking like this..."

"I smoke and you do other things."

He went to the window. "Like what, for instance?"

"You know perfectly well."

"Just say it. Say it loud and clear." The huddled pigeons at the gutter of the opposite building weren't moving at all.

"Okay," he said after a minute. "Okay. Okay."

They remained silent. The well-known sensation of calm settled in Satler and in order to loosen its grip he took her cup and carried it to the sink. She watched him from her stool, still smoking. The silence couldn't last. "Would you like something to eat?"

"To eat? Like what? What have we got?" He went to the fridge and opened it. "It's empty. There's nothing here."

"There's some cheese."

"Cheese? Cheese?" He opened the door compartment.

"Cheese spread."

"No, I don't want cheese spread. I'd rather wait and see what you bring back from the market. And anyway, I'm not hungry."

Silently she extinguished her cigarette. Then she went into the bathroom. He emptied the ash-tray and went to the bathroom door. "Okay, get some Bologna sausage, and some goat cheese, not the green one like the other day." She was brushing her teeth.

The mildew spot in the corner above the window had grown larger. There were crumbs of hardened tooth-paste in the wash-basin.

"Will you pick up a newspaper on your way back?"

"Why didn't you get one yourself?"

"It was too early. I told you I'd come only an hour ago." She didn't look at him. "Why on earth couldn't you bring me a newspaper? I was working all night..."

She started to comb her hair.

All right, he said to himself. All right. He knew how hard it was to make her speak up when she had decided not to. She went numb, as if this was a solution, instead of trying to talk it over.

He turned around, went to the bedroom and quietly took his clothes off. His pyjama jacket was under the pillow, but he couldn't find the trousers. He put his slippers on and went to the anteroom. Marika was donning her fur coat. "Have you any idea where my pyjama trousers are?"

"No."

There was nothing to be done here.

"Will you at least get me the damn newspaper?"

Suddenly he perceived that she was on a brink of tears. He thought of saying to her that she shouldn't cry outside since the tears would freeze on her face but he controlled himself. She seemed to brace herself as if she wanted to plunge into an attack, but when she spoke up it was in an almost normal voice. "Just leave me alone, please, just for once I don't want to talk it over!" Turning around, she opened the door and Satler asked himself whether he should dive and shut the door and lock it, but he didn't move. "You see, you did speak another word!" he cried. "That's how you keep your promises." She stepped out and closed the door. In the next moment it occured to him that the elevator was out of order. Aha, that would be another proof of his egotism. He was listening to her foot-steps. They stopped in front of the elevator for a minute, then started to descend. As soon as he couldn't hear them any more, he felt the old desire to run after her. He could buy some flowers in the market and try to find her. The cold would be deterring fruit-sellers and housewives alike and there wouldn't be the usual throng... But it was impossible... She was upset and she would resent every token of good will on his part. She would think that too was part of his strategy, hurting her and then taking it all back, as if nothing had happened... He went to the kitchen and, leaning against the window–pane with his brow, slanted his gaze downwards, but the lowest thing he could see in the sombre ravine was the second floor of the building opposite. He dragged the stool from the table and stepped up onto it. Now he could see the huddled winoes waiting in front of the drugstore at the other side of the street. A black car glided along the slippery road. And then everything was foggy and indiscernible as his breath had coated the pane.

Grabbing the window–handle with one hand and clinging to the window–post with the other, he pulled himself as high as he could. Here, the pane was clear. He didn't dare breathe. Since he had to stand on his toes he shook the slippers off. While they dropped onto the floor with a thud, the drugstore entrance opened. The winoes started to limp in, dragging their feet. It was seven o'clock. Marika should be down by now. Could it be that she had fallen on the slippery entrance stairs and now couldn't even get up?

At last he caught sight of her. With the short, wary steps of a child or an old woman she was crossing the street, headed towards the tobacconist or the newsagent. In spite of the fur coat she seemed worn–out and unhappy. Satler turned the handle and pushed the wing of the window out. The cold from outside rushed in as if sucked by a vacuum. Gazing down at the precipice Satler could still discern every bristling hair, dark against the frosty white of his insteps.

JANI VIRK

Translated by Lili Potpara

Jani Virk, born 1962 in Ljubljana, is at present editor-in-chief of one of the Slovenian dailies. He used to be a member of the former Yugoslav junior ski team and remained a sportsman ever since. Published a book of poems, a collection of essays, a novel 'Rahela' (1989) and two collections of short stories: 'Jump Over' (1987) and 'The Door' (1991). He translates from German.

THE DOOR

Of course it isn't true, as I was often accused then, that I was doing nothing in my life. If nothing else, twice a week I took the first workers' bus to Ljubljana, the 5:05. That in itself wasn't easy; nowadays I probably couldn't make it any more. The faces of my fellow passengers were blank and worn out, their clothes reminded me of rusty cages in the ZOO. I felt no sympathy whatsoever for them. Although my clothes often smelt of alcohol and puke, although my jeans had holes in the knees, although my purple velvet jacket had a broken zip and although the tongue had broken off my left sneaker months ago, I had absolutely nothing in common with them. You know, I'm a spiritual person. And that makes a lot of difference. I hated the people from the bus more than I was willing to admit even to myself. If I hadn't been afraid of solitude, I would have never had the feeling that we were close.

On those days I arrived in Ljubljana just before six. I strolled down Miklošičeva to Tromostovje, picked up a copy of the paper from the fresh pile in front of the newsagent's at the market, the seller was never there before half past six, and then had a coffee at the Albanian by the Ljubljanica. At quarter past seven I rolled up the paper, put it under my arm and headed for the Faculty of Theology.

My girl–friend didn't at all like the fact that I was attending the course in cosmology at the Theology. "This word sounds strange to me," she used to say. To tell the truth, she never knew what it meant. "Not only to you, it sounds strange to everybody," I was answering. I never added that there existed different levels of ignorance and strangeness. To some people strangeness can be very close. She was getting dissatisfied with me. Earlier she didn't care if I never went to the lectures at the Faculty of Arts, she herself encouraged me to neglect my studies and come to her when the kids in the kindergarten where she worked were asleep. I stopped counting how many times I laid her over the plushy teddy–bears in the toy–room and lifted her gown from behind. And now suddenly I was supposed to go to classes, although I had neglected them for at least two months. Or to find a part–time job. Or something else. Suddenly she was full of brilliant ideas about what I could do. Anything seemed appropriate than cosmology. When I finally asked her, in the middle of an argument on the way home from the movies, what cosmology meant, she was stubbornly silent for a few seconds, and then she scratched my hand, which was tangible proof of her rage. In such cases I was neither tender nor tolerant, also for her own good. Along with well aimed curses I tore the buttons off her lace blouse with a single pull in the middle of the street. She wasn't wearing a bra underneath (I'd said I disapproved before we left her rented flat, to no avail). At that moment half a dozen stupid lustful male eyes started staring at her naked breasts. I walked away, but she came running after me after a couple of seconds. She held the blouse tightly together with her hands. She pushed into me, I had to hold her by the shoulders. We were silent all the way to her car. As we drove towards her basement flat, she started to cry, and through the tears she sobbed that she could hate things even if she didn't know what they meant. Naive as I was, I realized that some day we might part. "Is it possible that a spiritual man and a non–spiritual woman can really love each other?", I was asking myself and felt enormous emptiness because I guessed the answer.

"Cosmology, cosmology", I sometimes whispered into her ear, later, when we were breathing hard on the plushy teddies, and she usually got so passionate that the straw in the teddies squeaked horribly. "Can wickedness with a positive aim be a reflection of spirituality?", I often wondered. "Does a positive aim exist at all?", I often wondered.

Every Monday and Wednesday, at seven twenty–five, I was in the lecture hall at the Theological. The faces of the people sitting all around me didn't look especially spiritual. I had a similar feeling among the pale, spotty faces of the students at the Faculty of Mechanical Engineering, where I went to a couple of lectures with a good friend of mine. Judging by his looks, the lecturer himself could pass as a conductor on a coach. He spoke about various theories concerning space, Ancient Greek, medieval and modern. He talked about the boundaries of space, atoms and emptiness within them, about the disintegration of space, the focal point, about millions and billions of years. He always strung his words together in a casual way, with the skilful rhetoric of an expert tired of talking about one and the same thing all the time. Some students were carefully making notes, sentences like "space was, as they say, created so and so many million years ago", "space is, as they say, this long and this wide", "some stars, as they say, no longer exist and still give light", "space is, as they say, measured in millions of years, a very unstable thing, and the question remains as to what is beyond its edge", others were getting ready for the next lecture, and yet others were reading magazines under the desk. Every now and then the lecturer yawned. Of course, measured in hours, it was still very early.

For weeks and weeks, twice every week, I sat in the lecture hall at the Theological from half past seven to nine, and floated in space with an open mind. Sometimes it so happened that I managed to retain the feeling for days and days, and finally it was enough to go to the lecture only once a week or even once a fortnight. My girl often accused me of being thrown out of the world. "You are thrown out of the world", she was saying, and I always imagined how we at one point were discovered in the kindergarten, on top of the teddies by the parents of the sleeping babies, and they threw me, small and shabby, through the window, and I started floating through the air, and light, hardly physical, rising higher and higher above the Earth and finally soaring into space.

The conflicts between us were getting more and more serious, and I was thinking of giving in, for the sake of peace, and, what was even more important, because she stopped lending me money and her car, which I, a boy from out of town, how shall I put it, often needed desperately. And then something happened which put a stop to my intentions.

One day, at half past seven sharp, a woman I'd never seen before appeared in the lecture hall at the Theological, and immediately after I'd spotted her went to sit in the first row by the window. The sun was rising above the roof of the neighbouring house, and was throwing light right where she sat. For a couple of moments I had a feeling that she had dispersed and was no longer there. Only later, after having gazed through the dispersed light, did I see her again. I often watch women I like. I know the delight of aesthetics and the delight of eroticism. However, what was then going on in the lecture hall at the Theological had nothing to do with delight. For an hour and a half, with a pleasant pain in my heart I fixedly gazed at the back and hair of the woman, whose name I didn't know, and whose face I'd never seen. "Eternity, space, black holes, explosions on the sun, collision of comets", the lecturer was saying, and his words were bouncing off my gaze and falling on the woman by the window.

After the lecture I pushed my way through the bored, spotty students to the exit, and on the stairs caught up with the woman from the first row. When I saw her face I experienced a moment of confusion. She was older than me, but I couldn't guess her age. There was a feature on her face, which was even more beautiful than I had imagined, which hid the years. Was she twenty- five, thirty or thirty-five? I invited her for a coffee and she accepted. "We can drink it at my place", she said. "I don't like cafes and the noise in them." As we walked along the empty streets she told me about her illness, because of which she couldn't come to the lectures. "Why do you go to these lectures anyway?" I asked her. She didn't answer. Did she hear me? I repeated the question. She never answered.

84

She lived on the third floor in an old house. We walked into a big room, full of old objects and cobwebs. A collapsible bed stood under the window and a dusty mirror hung on the opposite wall. Next to it was an old oak door with an iron latch, which looked like an entrance door. I thought it led to the bathroom or toilet, but she took the coffee pot and went to the corridor to fetch the water. "The toilet is outside", she said at the door.

Later we drank coffee and discussed cosmology. She spoke softly and slowly, and I didn't understand the smile on her face. She moved as if she were not physical, and she incited in me such a strong desire to touch her body that I could hardly control myself. She noticed my excitement and smilingly asked me if it wouldn't be better if I left. "Sure," I said and looked at my wrist where there was no watch, "it's time." I got up, said goodbye and slightly confused headed for the door with the iron latch.

"Not there," she said anxiously, and in the dusty mirror I saw her approach me. She took me by the hand and led me to the entrance door.

From that day on I again started attending the cosmology course regularly. My girl was threatening to finally get rid of me. "You are alienated, you are using me, you don't even come to the kindergarten any more," she was telling me. I didn't try to deny it. I myself didn't know why she bothered to stay with me. Apart from her car, which made my life easier, there was nothing she could still give me. All I was interested in was the woman from the lecture hall. Twice a week after the classes I went to her place for a coffee and we talked cosmology. We talked and talked, and I couldn't draw a line between spiritual and sexual attraction. She never gave me a hint that she could. And she never gave me a hint that she couldn't. When I started visiting her on the days when there were no cosmology classes she took it perfectly naturally. She was always home and it always seemed as if she was expecting me. And again and again, just before she sent me away, she uttered a sentence, which meant the most to me, and which I could never fully understand. "I can physically feel eternity," she was saying and smiling at me so that I had difficulties remaining seated on the chair. "Do you know what that means?", she was asking, leaning towards me, and with my gaze I could slide down her beautiful face behind her blouse, almost all the way down to her nipples.

All that I can remember from that period was my going to and leaving her place. The world and my life became transparent and unnecessary when I wasn't with her.

One day our conversation lasted till evening. When she leant towards me just before I planned to leave, and I saw the gentle swaying of her breasts, I could no longer control myself. I hugged her and slowly slid my hand behind her shirt. I touched her nipple, which was hard and rough, and it tickled my finger. She didn't move away, she was giving herself so gently and tenderly that I wondered whether I was really touching her or was it just my imagination. I got up and carried her to the bed. I slowly undressed her and pressed my face against her cold skin. She stroked my face and started undoing my buttons. We made love for a long time, late into the night.

"Go now," she said when we were through. I dressed, she took me by the hand and led me to the door. She unlatched it and let me go. I felt questions under my tongue. She kissed me on the cheek and opened the door. As I stepped through it, I saw her face in the dusty mirror. Then I stepped into the void. And fell. I heard a gentle slam of the door behind me. Back down I fell, and I could see the sky full of stars. I heard a bang, as if a bird's wing had snapped in the vicinity. And for a moment I could feel eternity in the air. And...

ROŠLIN AND VERJANKO

I met Verjanko when I was twelve. We played football together for the parish school, and he was the only one to now and then pass an odd ball to me, a newcomer. He was some years older than I, four or five, I don't know. He was being trained to become a carpenter, and his big wish was to build a huge closet–maze in the room he shared with his brother. At his place I got drunk for the first time, smoked the first cigarette and saw the first porn magazine. The first time I saw a completely naked woman (his mother, who, on a summer night, just as I was sneaking out of Verjanko's room, came totally and absolutely naked from her bedroom and slapped me, a fourteen year old, so strongly that her huge breasts swayed like bells in the room). It was Verjanko's fault that I had to repeat the second year of grammar school and it was also his fault that I got so deeply involved in drugs that the usual connections in my mind simply got disengaged and connected anew in an utterly impossible way: when I played basketball I thought of graveyards, when I was supposed to sleep with a woman I thought of basketball, and when I thought of death I was dying of laughter.

Then came completely different times. That summer, when I graduated from grammar school and was getting ready to go to the army, Verjanko, a skilled carpenter by that time, went to join his father in Germany. We wrote letters to each other for some time, but they were getting shorter and shorter and one day finally stopped coming altogether. I managed to get through the army – I acquired a pretty bad opinion of people – and disappointed with the entire world returned home. I changed, I started reading books and writing down various impressions and thoughts. I wrote fictitious speeches and letters, and became so withdrawn that the whole of space together with the people were squeezed into my head. I was sending articles to various magazines, and some nihilist student paper, among various cynicisms and obscenities, even published my perfectly serious article entitled God's Insomnia and Loss of the Penultimate Hope. I can still remember the main point of the discussion, which I could briefly summarize as follows: God cannot sleep. His wakefulness is so total that nothing whatsoever can escape him. And because he sees and knows everything, he cannot overlook the simple fact that there are a lot of ignoramuses, fools and good- for–nothings among people. And so it's perfectly clear to him that it would be totally senseless and totally against his goodwill to let the ignoramuses, fools and good–for–nothings stay what they are for ever. So he abolishes eternity, which is indivisible, and therefore the entire human race loses it. He keeps it for his private use, for his eternal wakefulness, which is just as good to him as a TV switched on by itself, watching itself in the mirror. God knows it, and even if he were a man, he still wouldn't be able to sleep.

The fact was that I couldn't sleep. Every night I was awake in my bed, reading, looking through the window, and emptying bottles of wine, carefully taking care not to let my consciousness escape into sleep. In the mornings I fell asleep when no shadow remained of the night.

I enroled in philosophy and soon realized that I could improve my life with its help. I figured out that I had to direct all my abilities into obsessions, which I had been till then too shyly hiding within myself. I became strong and slightly nasty. I was digging into people and jerking the rug out from under them, with women I was creating painful relationships for them, and educated myself into a real bastard.

When I was studying for finals at the end of the first year, Verjanko returned from Germany. The boy had a thick mustache, and his once so natural clumsiness had changed into a harmonious elegance, under which I immediately spotted a lot of empty space which could be used. He drove to my place in his father's Mercedes. He didn't touch the wine I offered. We chatted about the events of the past few years. After a while he became nervous, but I wasn't going to help him and was pretending although I knew he wanted to ask me a favour. I was pulling his leg, and when he finally told me what he had on his mind I acted generous.

The problem was that Verjanko's father, who was supposed to stay in Germany for two more years, learned that his wife was being unfaithful to him. He didn't want to lose her and the recently renovated house. So Verjanko and he agreed they would, under the pretence of my having nowhere to go (I had a fight with my parents), get me to live with Verjanko's mother as a spy-tenant. I quite liked the plan, because Verjanko offered me a couple of hundred marks a month for the favour. However, I moaned and tried to make Verjanko believe that I was doing him an enormous favour, which was in conflict with my moral principles, and as such, too badly paid. Verjanko understood and generously assured me that money was no problem, since his father was willing to pay a lot more if I wanted. Which I did.

The next day after lunch I went to see Verjanko. His mother made coffee and flattered me that I had grown into a real man in the years she hadn't seen me. She, at forty-three, was anything but a faded woman, and with a pleasant feeling I remembered the slap from so many years ago. (Yes, madam, I said, women don't slap me any more – she got the hint and smiled not at all shyly – but life does). I started moaning about the argument with my parents, about my impossible situation and how I'd been unsuccessfully sending ads to papers to find a room. Without any special sympathy the mother observed that life was a miserable delusion and there was nothing to be done about it, and Verjanko acted generous and offered me his room as a makeshift solution; he didn't need it while he was working with his father in Germany. His mother pointed out that he would have to talk to his father about it, hoping he would object to unnecessary renting; he hardly knew me and by no means needed extra money. Verjanko suggested he could phone him in Germany the same evening and ask what he thought. That was the end of the discussion and Verjanko and I went out. He happily patted me on the shoulder and bought me a drink in a nearby bar.

A week later (a day before Verjanko left for Germany) I was already a tenant. Madam received me cautiously, with a judging eye. That night we had a two–purpose party: we were celebrating my moving in and Verjanko's departure. Verjanko's brother and his wife came for dinner and nobody had much fun.

When I woke up the following morning, Verjanko was already on his way. His mother called me from work and asked me to hang out the washing, since she learned she had a seminar somewhere by the sea over the weekend (sure, Ema, sure, don't you worry). I hung out the washing and made sure that the enormous breasts I saw when I was fourteen weren't the product of exaggerated childish imagination. Around noon I went on my errands, and when I got back, Ema's suitcases were already waiting in the hall. I wanted to go to my room, but she called me to the kitchen and offered me a coffee. She thanked me for hanging out the washing, and I told the truth when I said I did it with great pleasure. A car honked in front of the house, she got up, looked through the window, leaned towards me and pinched me in the cheek. (This month you are here for free, look after the house and don't pee in the bed, she was saying to me as if to a child.)

Her weekend lasted until Wednesday. In the meantime I emptied half of the house's wine cabinet, lay in Ema's bed and watched TV, studied a little and phoned whoever I could think of. Ema returned fresh as a twenty–five year old, and it seemed that the seminar had been successful. She greeted me with a kiss on the lips, and I clung to her like an old lover. Before she had time to get surprised I licked her lips. She grabbed my bum and stuck her tongue into my mouth. She threw me on the floor and got on top of me. (I'm the only one to know how many times I dreamt about lascivious women, but Ema was the first and the only one I met.)

The following months I devoted myself to two main things. I studied like never before, and at night, during the day, in the bathroom, on the parquet, in the boiler room, against the walls with flowery wall-papers, satisfied Ema. I was hanging out her washing, cooking lunches, driving her on trips, making her forget her lover and spending the enormous quantities of money her husband was sending me. A feeling rose in me, which compared to what I'd felt about Ema's buttocks, her excited pubic region and her never squeezed enough breasts, was something entirely different. (Ema will also die one day, her body will disintegrate into primordial substance, her juices will flow to the nearest underground stream or lake, and she will scream in a completely different way. God will block his ears, but won't be able to do anything, stars will bump into each other and nobody will see it. Ema saw it.) We never discussed emotions, we were content with the common – animal-like – thought that one should first provide for oneself, without choosing too moralistic means, and above all, survive till the end.

At Christmas Verjanko and his father came home for two weeks. I reported to them that everything was fine with Ema, and that it was unlikely she had a lover. Under the pretence I was going on a winter vacation I went home for a couple of days.

It was difficult without Ema, and I couldn't wait to hear from her that her husband and son had left. Every night I looked at the photos of Ema naked, which I had taken from every possible position: I was lying on the floor and Ema stepped over me, I was squatting before her chair and took a picture of her cunt, I was sitting on the closet and caught her lying with her legs spread wide in the bed. The very hour they left I was already lying next to Ema, while they were probably discussing their wise decision about having Ema watched and were in their minds already at the doorstep of a brothel by the Frankfurt railway station. Then followed two surprises. I was moved into the sitting room, because Verjanko started carrying out his teenage plan – the maze (a massive network of beams was spread all over the room, and a narrow shelf for sleeping was fixed onto the wall in the corner), and: Ema wanted to get a divorce and have a baby by me.

In February Ema got pregnant. Her lust became more polished and refined. She was on sick leave for weeks and weeks, and played with me. She was indefatigable, she never had enough, so I didn't have enough time to study.

In April Verjanko came home for ten days and completed his maze with an iron framework and massive boards. He didn't let anybody into the room, he was rather cold towards me (maybe he suspected or knew something), but I had enough aces up my sleeve, so I didn't have to hide my contempt.

In June Ema changed. Her belly grew, she was tender and mother-like. Most nights we slept peacefully next to each other, she told me she loved me a lot, which we had known for a long time anyway.

In August Ema got a divorce and her husband brought a groundless action against me. Ema promised she would never cheat on me and granted me absolute freedom.

In September Ema and I got married. Three days after the wedding we had twins.

In November Verjanko came back home. Ema and I let him stay the night in the sitting room. We locked the door of the bedroom and left the balcony door ajar.

I woke up in this dark room. For three days I have been bumping into wooden barriers, desperately looking for an exit. When I'm tired, I climb onto the wooden shelf and by torch-light read the book On Good Manners which Verjanko had brought into this idiotic maze together with me. With the razor that Verjanko left me I cut out individual letters and glue them on the floor with my saliva. I have glued a lot already, and I'm tired. I will glue these now: I don't regret anything, but it didn't last long enough and I miss Ema now. God, if you can see this, please bite through Verjanko's throat, and then give eternal life to everybody despite everything. I'm already dead.

Rošlin

REGATTA

"No wonder she left me," I was thinking during a walk along the coast, a few days after the woman I'd spent the last four years with finally walked out on me. I was wondering whether despite all the love I felt for her I hadn't secretly wanted her to leave me, so that I could fall from her protective arms through the layers of the world into life as it really was: dispersed, unsure, with no hope of holding on to it. I walked down the sandy beaches, watching the lovers hugging in the light of the setting sun. I never used to do it, just as I never gave my woman the feeling of safety. I also didn't know how to show her how much I loved her, or that I wanted to keep her by my side in my own special way. So she left.

And I walked along the sandy beach and further down to the sharp rocks, waves splashing against them. On my back I carried my rucksack and sleeping bag, in my hand I held a wooden stick I'd picked up from the sea. I was headed for nowhere, I missed nothing, regretted nothing. I dodged the sharp edges of the rocks and every now and then looked at the sea. The red setting sun was throwing a grim light over some fishing boats. An old, tired swimmer was swimming along the coast. I walked, looking for a quiet isolated bay where I could spread my sleeping bag and spend the night. The nearby tourist town was filled with holiday makers, and the beaches were invaded by couples making love to the humming of the waves. I was bored by their sighs, I tried to avoid them as I walked, the animal–like deep breathing of men and falsetto shrieks of women in the tiny bays among the rocks were making me laugh. I had to walk for a long time before I'd left behind all the kneaded, sweaty human bodies, and reached an abandoned stone fisherman's house. I pushed aside the ramshackle door and stepped inside. There was nothing inside, only a torn fisherman's net hanging on a wooden beam. I pulled it on the floor, spread some clothes and the sleeping bag over it and so fixed a pleasant bed for myself. I took some two–day–old bread and the thermos bottle with fresh water from the rucksack, and went to sit in front of the house. Leaning against it I looked across the sea, at the narrow bright line of the horizon, and into the sky, where the first stars had started glittering. My gaze fed on the centuries old rays, I was breathing centuries old air. With my teeth I was tearing two–day old bread and drank tepid stale water. Warm wind was pleasantly blowing across my bare, tired feet. Crickets were singing in the bushes behind the house. Waves were splashing into the rocks, and I was listening to the wet, muffled sliding of the sand along the rocks. I walked to the water and stepped into it. The waves threw sand and little pebbles onto my feet. I stood there for a while, without thoughts, looking into the distance. "All this is so unreal, and it's only an illusion that I exist and that I'm here," I thought later. "This scene has been repeated times without number, and it is at this very moment being repeated in countless other galaxies. I'm not here and I'm not there," I was thinking. "I'm everywhere and nowhere," I said to myself and went to bed. "My life ended a long time ago," I thought just before I fell asleep.

In the morning I left all my stuff in the little house and set off through the bushes to find some food. I found a fig grove, took off my shirt, tied the sleeves together and picked the fruit into it. When I started for the house again, a dirty dog sneaked up on me from somewhere and kept barking behind me. I stoically tolerated its treacherous barking for a while. When we reached the bushes I put the figs aside and threw a couple of stones at it. I hit it with one, although I only wanted to scare it. It howled with pain, and for a moment I felt pity for it. I picked up the figs and walked on. On the way I also picked up some dry branches.

Two naked women lay on the rocks in front of the house. At first I could see only a leg on the rock, and for a second I thought the sea had washed up a human body. Only after a few steps did I see that the leg was resting on the rock in a relaxed straddle. I stopped and looked at the two young naked bodies. The girls were foreigners, about twenty years old. One had long black hair, the other was a blonde with hair cut very short. When they saw me they got scared. The dark one put her legs together and threw a towel over her body. I stepped towards them, dropped a couple of figs from the shirt into their laps and walked into the house. I waited, I thought they would leave. But they stayed right there in front of the house. And I stayed in the house. I had no watch, I didn't need a watch, but an odd hour passed before the door opened and the dark one, naked as before, peeked in. She moved her hand to her mouth and said: "Mangiare?" I knew what it meant, so I pointed at the figs, which were still in the shirt. "Prendi," I said.

"A, ti parli Italiano?" she asked, opened the door wide and stepped over the thresh-hold. The sun threw some light between her legs and tiny drops of sweat glistened on her pubic hair.

"No," I answered and pointed at the figs again.

She explained to me that they wanted no more figs, but were inviting me out to have a snack with them. I refused, but she insisted. She called her friend, they surrounded me, naked, and tried to talk me into coming out. I was wondering whether to take my things and leave. I didn't want any company. They claimed I was too thin, although I'd never been too thin, and, laughing, were asking me if I was homosexual. "I've had enough problems with myself in my life even without being gay," I was thinking to myself, but I never answered. They pushed the matter for so long that I finally gave in and walked out with them. From the ice bag they took sandwiches and beer and offered me some. I took a can of beer and a sandwich. The rocks were white with the midday heat, I brought the sleeping bag from the house and spread it over them. With naked chest and bare feet I lay on the bag wearing my jeans. The two women laughed and asked me why I didn't take my clothes off. They brought their air mattresses to me and lay on either side of me. They were teasing me, and I kept more or less quiet. I put the sandwich on my belly, my hand under my head and slowly sipped the beer. Every now and then I glanced at their naked bodies. They lay on their hips and talked over me. I could sense their smell. They were beautiful, young and attractive. They glistened with cocoa tanning lotion, and wanted to spread some on me. I didn't let them. They placed stones on me and touched me, laughing. I liked it, but at the same time I wanted to be left alone. "This is an illusion," I was saying to myself, "just like everything is an illusion." I sipped my beer and peered into the shiny sun. Dark circles started appearing in front of my eyes. "Too much light brings darkness," I concluded philosophically, and closed my eyes. The women started teasing me even more provocatively, but I never responded and didn't open my eyes. They soon got bored, and after a while I heard them dabbling in the water. The world around me moved further and further away, the landscape rose in whirls, space became emptier and emptier, I was sinking into sleep.

When I awoke, they were no longer there. I sat up, the sandwich and the stones they had placed on me fell off me. The sun had burnt me, I was reddish all over; the skin remained white only where the sandwich and the stones had been. My head was spinning, I undressed and waded into the water to get cool. I dived under the surface and touched stones at the bottom of the sea. Shoals of fish whizzed around me, algae wrapped around my hands.

Then I went into the house and till evening stared at the sea through the window. The sun was sinking deeper and deeper into it, the red colour spreading over the horizon. In the evening I went looking for worms for fish bait. I took off the wooden door, and got some transparent plastic thread and hooks from the rucksack. With difficulty I carried the door to the sea, threw it into the water, lay on top and paddled away from the shore with my hands. There were some fishing boats out in the sea, but I stopped before I reached them. I waited for a long time until I caught the first big fish. When I'd caught another one, I returned to the shore. I made a fire with the branches I picked in the morning and roasted the fish.

The two Italians didn't come the next day. I spent the day alone, without seeing anybody.

I would also have spent the following day alone, if the water shortage hadn't forced me to walk into the town. The streets and cafes were swarming with tourists; I was fed up with their faces, which looked happy only because they'd heard somewhere that one was supposed to be happy when on holiday. I had a little money left in my pocket; I'd left behind all that I had scooped up in my life. After a long search I found a shop where I was able to buy a five-litre water bottle. I paid the last of my money for it. That was all right. I didn't need it. In a sweet-shop I forced my way to the toilet through the tourists stuffing themselves with cakes or neatly queuing up in front of the ice-cream machine, and filled my bottle with water. Then I returned to my house. On the way I scratched my hand badly on a bush, and a huge fly kept landing on the wound. I waved my arm to force it away. It wouldn't be forced away. We were finally separated by the door I closed behind me.

Every few days I went into town to get water. I didn't miss anything. I roasted the fish I caught in the evenings, ate the fruit I picked in the fields and groves in the mornings. During the day I spread my sleeping bag and clothes over the rocks around the house, and nobody came near me. I spent most of the time lying in the house, staring through the window or at stone walls. I didn't think about anything, and if I did, I tried to imagine emptiness. It calmed me down, and I felt I was falling through the layers of the world.

One day, leaving the town with my bottle in my hand, I spotted a friend from secondary school in the crowd across the street. We looked at each other and he stepped towards me. I didn't want to stop, I nodded in recognition and wanted to walk on. He took me by the arm.

"Do you remember me?" he asked.

"I do," I said and freed my arm from his grip.

97

He asked me to go for a drink. I refused, I didn't need a drink, I had five litres of fresh water in my bottle. However, he somehow made me go with him to the pier. He told me he was there with his uncle, aunt and their two daughters, and that they needed somebody to complete the crew for a night regatta, since the women didn't want to do it. The regatta was to start the following evening. With difficulty, as though my tongue would not obey me any longer, I explained to him that I knew nothing whatsoever about sailing. He assured me there was nothing to it, and that all I needed to do was help hoist and roll the sails. I didn't feel like helping anybody hoist and roll sails. I shook my head and looked at the sea. Wind was blowing, waves were wrinkled over the surface. Suddenly I could smell the scent of the open sea, for a moment I was overwhelmed by the picture of the endless azure of the sea. "It would actually be very nice," I thought, "if I could look anywhere and always see the sea. And see depths below me, my gaze getting lost in them."

"I might come," I said.

He wanted me to say I would definitely come. This I couldn't promise. He wanted to touch my conscience, he dug into it with the reproach that he and his uncle wouldn't be able to take part in the regatta if they didn't have a third man. That was none of my business, and had nothing to do with my conscience. Before I left I asked him where to come if I decided to, and he told me.

The whole of the next day I spent lying around in my little house, watching the sea through the door. The wind was blowing and making waves. For hours and hours I observed their rhythm, which was moving into me. My thoughts were far away from me, my body became light, trembling with a hardly noticeable feeling of happiness.

Towards evening I gathered all my things into the rucksack and said good-bye to the house. The wind was strong, heavy clouds hung in the sky. The coast was deserted. I didn't know what the time was, I wasn't sure whether the people waiting for me were already or no longer at the appointed place.

When I approached the marina, my friend came running towards me.

"My uncle is getting impatient," he said, turned away and quickly walked towards the marina. I didn't keep up with his pace, I was in no hurry. Every now and then he looked over his shoulder, stopped, waited for me and then again quickened his pace, thinking he would make me walk faster.

His uncle greeted me on the boat with unpleasant nervous kindness. He squeezed my hand, helped me get my rucksack off, virtually pulled it off, and then, with competitive haste, alien to me, suggested we spread and roll up the sails a couple of times to practice. Unwillingly I cooperated, he encouraged me, actually, rudely demanded to do something faster which I considered senseless and superfluous. With nervous haste he kept repeating that "we have to stay in the lead", that right after the start "we must keep up with the leaders." After we had lifted and lowered the sails a couple of times, he took me down the stairs to the narrow cabin of the boat, repeating that we should work harder during the regatta. He showed me the navigation equipment and pointed to the berths at both sides of the tiny room: "If there's any time, you can lie down at the back. The front should be loaded as little as possible."

There was only a little time left before the regatta was to start, and we went to a nearby restaurant. With the boasting gestures of a rich businessman my former friend's uncle gave his order to the waiter. He urged me to eat something myself, but I lied that I had already eaten. Nervously and greedily he ate his steak, and with the enthusiasm of a bad amateur talked about the coming regatta. I took a piece of bread from the basket and slowly nibbled on it. Every now and then I looked at his fat face, spoilt by luxury, and the pieces of steak he was carelessly pushing into his mouth. I was sick of looking at him and his nephew, who was neatly cutting his fried cheese. I was looking at the gloomy sky. A storm was coming on.

When the boat sailed out of the marina I felt relieved. The evening was turning into night, heavy gray clouds hung threatening above the sea. The air was thick and tense, it started thundering, at first some heavy, big drops fell, and then it started pouring with rain. For a while we could still see the other boats, but soon we were alone on the rough sea. There was darkness all around us; every now and then it was brightened by lightning shooting into the sea. The owner of the boat screamed that we had lost our competitors and that one of them was surely in front of us. He wanted to unroll an additional sail, the spinnaker, as he called it, but I didn't even think of crawling to the stem of the inclined boat with my former friend to do it. I was sitting by the man shouting stupidly, holding onto the metal rail. Then the man let me steer and went to roll out an additional sail with his nephew. When they pulled it up, the stormy wind violently caught in it and the boat moved dangerously to the side. In the dark, in between the lightning, I could see both men clutching at the rail. I let the steering wheel go and grabbed the rail, which stuck out high above the sea. The rail on the other side was almost in the sea; the waves were constantly covering it. Water was pouring into the cabin, I thought we would sink. However, the men at the mast somehow managed to pull down the extra sail, and the water no longer flowed so forcibly into the boat. They crawled back to the steering wheel, the businessman leaned over the back of the boat and threw up. Then he went to the cabin and returned with life-jackets. He told me there was a lot of water in the cabin. I didn't care. I felt good in the storm, I liked the scenes when the lightning brightened the sea. The businessman went back to the cabin and came back to tell us we were sailing in the right direction. "Some three more hours, and we'll reach the lighthouse," he said. "We must be among the first." Then he took over from me at the wheel. I put on the life-jacket and held the rail. The waves were crashing into the boat, every now and then it was immersed in a bigger wave, rain was pouring incessantly from the stormy clouds. Hours passed, sinking deeper and deeper into the night. The storm never eased, it was moving across the sea together with us. The businessman peered senselessly into the dark, looking for his competitors. Two or three times more he threw up; during one of his attacks of sickness lightning struck in the vicinity, I could see pieces of meat falling from his mouth.

The businessman was growing more and more restless. By his calculations we should already have reached the lighthouse. He crawled into the cabin and back again, and constantly repeated that our heading was right, but that something had to be wrong. Soon he could no longer hide his fatigue. With difficulty he clutched the wheel and at times shouted "ship, shore, lighthouse," but nothing happened. Only the night and the sea and right above us the clouds. His nephew also held the rail with the last of his strength and repeated after him "ship, shore, lighthouse." Soon the businessman could soon no longer hold the wheel, and I took over. He sat down by his nephew, and with stronger thrusts of the waves they could hardly manage to stay on the leaning boat.

I felt nice in the middle of the rough sea, my eyes rested in the dark. I liked the wetness of the rain and the sea. I felt the soft depths below me.

I watched the businessman and his nephew's hand slide off the rail when the wind blew stronger. I let go of the wheel and tried to help them into the cabin. I myself had to take care not to fall into the sea. It was all right with the nephew, but the businessman resisted, confused, looking into the darkness, constantly repeating "lighthouse, lighthouse, lighthouse." I forcibly pulled him away from the rail and pushed him down the stairs into the interior of the boat.

Then I left the wheel and went to sit on the bow. The waves were splashing over my body. For a long time I looked quietly into the dark. Suddenly I heard a crack, louder than the humming of the storm and waves. I felt a push, the boat violently moved to both sides a couple of times and finally came to a standstill. I climbed off, and along the reefs washed by the sea reached a small island. The lighthouse stood on it. But it wasn't blinking. I got closer. I pushed aside the ramshackle door and stepped inside. I lay on the pile of dry algae and sank into a deep, peaceful sleep.

LELA B. NJATIN

Translated by Anne Čeh
"Why Do These Black Worms" translated by Krištof Jacek Kozak

Lela B. Njatin is the author's pen-name. Born 1963 in Ljubljana, she studied comparative literature and philosophy. Published a novel 'Intolerance' (1988). Included in an anthology 'Schellstrasse, Fernlicht' (DroschlVerlag Graz, Austria, 1991). Close to the Neue Slowenische Kunst circle she developed an authentic and independent author's voice which created, besides literature, many screenplays for video, film and comics. She also designed clothes and costumes for the theatre. She supports herself by writing for newspapers.

THE DEAD PERPETUALLY DREAM THE TRUTH (WINGS OF DESIRE OVER LJUBLJANA)

i am struggling through the forest with difficulty. the undergrowth is dense and the ground so soaked that i am sinking up to my ankles in mud. as i part the branches of the bushes i frighten a white dove. it flies up low over my head, to seat itself within arm's reach. i stretch out for it, it moves along, i leap towards it. it flutters some metres away. i hunt it so enthusiastically that i do not feel the boughs whipping my body and the thorns scratching my face. tomaž peers out of the trees and i wave to him. "i'm in hurry" and i rush after the dove. as i catch it it changes into a fish, slithering out of my hands to slip along the mud. it is impossible to follow. i return to the paved path that runs through the park in the shape of a star.

whilst awaiting for the signal at the traffic lights, matej is already standing there on the other side. it is hot, beads of perspiration are collecting beneath my leather cap and my leather jumpsuit sticks to my thighs. as i cross the road the light is becoming unbearable. it extends, to undermine objects and broaden space. the road becomes the widest take-off strip and the traffic light the control tower. the longer i walk towards the other side, the further it retreats. i stop, turn and gaze on all sides. the absence of aircraft hurts. my pilot's clothing is burning, strangely, shamefully, despairingly. the light is rancid, harsh, smothering. i slip off the leather gauntlets, undo my boots, pull the cap off my head. to myself, i imagine: but angels don't fly. they are everywhere, safeguarding every living creature so that each can go its own way.

matej grins at me from the other side. i hurry. he's far off but somehow i catch him up. he points to the wings on my back, the lumps of mud on them are more or less dry, though still clinging to the feathers: "let's go and have a drink". i become aware of the incredible wall beneath which we are standing. i glance upwards but nowhere is its end in sight. i lean right back but it merely seems as if there is some kind of tower at the top: conical, losing itself in infinity. returned to the other side of the take-off strip, i would certainly be able to tell what kind of structure it was. it would however, be extremely arduous. the light is all heat. and matej is here. but there must be a door somewhere, and the door has to be at ground level. i take a step but matej holds me back: "we are going in the other direction".

it blinds me. i pull out my glasses, putting them on. matej presses his lids together too. the image of the conical top does not vanish, perhaps it's a cathedral? i shall have to return alone to find out.

the otherwise short street is lengthening and lengthening. throughout we are walking alongside the high, windowless wall, and the sun hangs mercilessly above us, it has driven away all shade and chased beneath the leather tent of my flying suit, downwards over my thighs, squelchingly collecting in my boots. now the rivulets of sweat run from my brow to the bridge of my nose, pouring over the lower rim of my glasses, there to become droplets. with my thoughts i attempt to move our aim, and realize that the buildings in the distance are different from usual. matej and i exchange glances. he too is astonished.

there are poplars before us and a group of tiny houses. the heat is not so great and the air flows lighter. the pub we enter is pleasantly gloomy. now the water beneath my clothing is cool and i mop myself with the velour underside of my cap.

"so you don't believe in angels," matej begins the conversation.

"nothing exists that could fly, everything is fixed to the earth," i reply.

"i'm really interested as to how you can live so – terrestrially. you are actually completely equipped for flying," he indicates the wings i am flexing and shaking the mud off the feathers.

"you don't understand, these are the wings of desire. my aircraft is in ceaseless construction, my pilot equipment will be worn out with walking and be destroyed by windlessness."

the smile does not vanish from matej's face. he is a child of daedalus, believes we fell from the sky because of mistakes; human, divine – it's irrelevant to him, what's important is the availability of the sky, he never denies himself that.

"there's no place for cleaning here!" the waitress appears brusquely at our table.

i apologize. her expression surprises me much more than her sudden appearance. her face is somewhat different from those i am used to, actually it is similar but with a different expression that i can not define. despite the disgust, anger is indiscernible upon it, although favour far away...

"what do you want?!" she grouses.

and her figure – as if, were i to describe her, i require fresh words, nothing foreign but taken from this language, only different, above all differentiating, independent ones.

after he has ordered, matej pulls a metal cigarette case from out of his jacket, gazing round the pub for a light. he never carries any matches on him, is this his way of searching for angels? and the faces of the men in the inn are new to me too, wrinkled as in old men and thus perhaps seeming gloomy, nevertheless certainly not friendly. so unfriendly that matej remains seated. all of them are in dark suits with mourning ribbons on their lapels and the glasses are lost in their gigantic, cracked palms. they stare piercingly at us, although wordless i do not remember whether or not they were talking when we entered. the dusk in the room seemed to me full of tiny barbs and i sense most of them in the throats of these men. matej lays his cigarette down on the table, "let's change the subject."

"we are conversing with them now," i say.

i sense that the men's stares shorten, at the same time the barbs from the room thrust into me. death. a theme too simple to discuss with matej. to him this is probably a metaphysical state. precisely so: beyond. the two of us are silent.

"let's go." i drug us out of the pub. as we are leaving we frighten the ravens before the door. matej's smile has died down. the lighthaired youth is full of embarrassment because he has disturbed the sorrow of the seven with his own vitality and, for an instant, the thought occurs to me that i too have offended their severity with my own grotesque presence.

"death always provokes anger," i say to calm him.

he shrugs his shoulders, "shall we go elsewhere?"

"to talk? you have seen that life is mute."

he grins again. spreading his arms wide he shrieks, "death is mute! life is the story of all stories!"

the same words? the same pictures? the same meaning? again the light is as dense as milk. entangled in the humidity it creeps onto my skin like slime. i close my zips and pull up my straps, still always gazing in the direction where the heat of the mist has melted matej. the warm is damp. my leather wrappings soften into a pliable skin. i go down the steps to the river. tomaž is waiting for me. "are you an angel now? i ask him. "i am a dead person," he replies.

i sense the sounds from the zenith. when i lift my gaze a humming begins. high above my head creeps an aeroplane. from its tail a banner unfurls and balloons fall in vivid colours. whilst i am attempting to read the inscription, bells from the cathedral engulf the aircraft...

this tale, which occurred near the crossroads of šubičeva and titova in november 1987, is recorded with the assistance of boštjan seliškar, tomaž hostnik and ivan cankar.

INTOLERANCE (A FRAGMENT)

i open my eyes. srečko is asleep with his head right next to mine, lying on his back. a bent leg prays upwards from beneath the eiderdown he is clutching to his chest with both hands. he has pouted his full lips so that they are even more luscious and i have to kiss them.

throwing on a shirt, i unplug the grinder and drop the coffee into the water boiling on the stove. i set the coffee pot aside, mix in the coffee and boil it up again. i laugh when i spy my own face in the silver plated tray. i cover it with the cloth. i take two saucers and coffee cups from the cupboard, setting them with ham. i stack it all on the tray, adding a glass of milk. tray in hand i shuffle my feet over to my shoes and slip into them.

at the door out of the kitchen i come to a halt, astonished, "who are you?" i grate.

a group of men are peering around the room. one of them stops and gazes severely at me. another is staring at the picture above the fireplace, a third is opening the curtain at the window. "oh!" he wonders at what he has seen in the courtyard. the burial-ground is surrounded by a high wall which protects it from the curious.

"what are you doing here?" i ask again. the man who had stopped turned to me again, gestured to the other two and they depart.

in the evening, when srečko is seated at the monitor and i am reading, a young girl enters without knocking. she too inspects the room, wordlessly entering the bathroom, returning to direct herself towards the kitchen.

i serve her, angrily, "what do you want? how dare you come in here!"

she moves aside and continues on her way.

i hiss to srečko, "this flat's no longer ours!"

srečko nonchalantly stubs out a cigarette.

i am taken aback by this.

the girl returns.

"get out! out! and don't dare come back!" i push her out of the door.

"you didn't have to do that." srečko is unhappy.

"what? don't you care whether strangers promenade around this flat as if it were theirs?" i marvel.

"i do not know why you always have to be so unfriendly!"

"they are invading our privacy!"

"every little thing seems to threaten you!" he rises, unplugging the computer.

i seize held of his hand, "it really doesn't bother you?!"

he shakes me off, "you explain things to yourself in your own way. not everything happens within the scope of your comprehension! Other people may think other things important. you ought to apologize to them," he slams the door behind him.

i sense how the lead shot speeds through my veins. my lungs feel like a cement block and i sense charred skin on my cheeks. i stagger towards the yard. a deathly silence is suspended between the walls. the motionless bodies on the tombstones are still resting, eyelids lowered. i do the rounds of the windows and whisper, "guard my dwelling." i follow srečko.

when i return, drawers from the cupboard are lying everywhere, their contents spilled out all over the floor, the table overflowing with glasses and empty bottles, remains of food and ash scattered around it, open books on the armchairs, the standard lamp overturned, panes in the window smashed...i rush out into the yard: the tombs are empty.

i sense a tingling in my hands. i lift my palms: the skin is bursting and the flesh erupts before my eyes. the wounds heal with extraordinary speed and the skin that had flaked off alters into scales. i shake them off, in horror, and run away.

INTOLERANCE
(ANOTHER FRAGMENT)

"at rest!" commands the lieutenant.
i collapse onto the ground. my eyes are sore from the concentrated staring into the forest. beware of every leaf that trembles, every shadow that moves. walk rapidly but inaudibly, finger on the trigger. the base of my neck has petrified and my knees are stiff from the persistent tension. i am prepared to shoot at any rustle not in the context of forest.

i roll onto my back with difficulty. the glaring sky blinds me. my comrades have sat down, are unbuttoning shirts, rolling up their sleeves and fastening their thick overcoats across their rucksacks, around the hips, flinging the into the empty ammunition chest. lighting cigarettes, they are gesturing with billycans full of spirits, stuffing themselves with the food given to them in the village. laughing, they are shouting at the tops of their voices. for them it is all over. someone has flung away the stinking soles of his boots.

the lieutenant is peering round. deciding upon the hayhouse full of hay, he makes his way towards it. "some help. lads!" his delighted voice is to be heard. some of them rush over. they start to guffaw and push an automobile out from beneath the hay.

"nice war trophy," someone says.

"isn't it rather compulsory requisition in times of peace?" someone else responds.

Intolerance (Another Fragment)

this seems like a marvellous joke to them all.

"comrades, we shall drive to freedom as the dignified victors," the lieutenant thumps his chest ceremoniously.

i am unable to hold my head up in my palms any longer and drop again. again that empty sky with the penetrating light. i close my eyes. they rest. my neck rests. the ground is softening my bones. i lie in pieces. perhaps there really won't be anything more. perhaps all of them have already fled, perhaps the people's courage grew and they have killed them themselves, with their bare hands. after all it would be the masses against the few and freedom lay at their feet. they could at least have hunted them and imprisoned them. that way they would not escape justice. i can't rid myself of my anxiety. the forest is vast, capable of concealing anything.

"there!" i screech, aiming my rifle.

my companion stare.

a courier crawls out of the bushes.

i begin to shake. i might have killed him. my comrades laugh at me, their fearless voices are loathsome.

the lieutenant taps me on the shoulder.

"calm down! everything is over now, tomorrow you'll be home. perhaps then you will believe the victory is ours!"

"comrade lieutenant," the courier is getting his breath back, »unfortunately you are not going home just yet."

speechless heads turn towards him.

"you must take the gang that is threatening the village."

in an instant my anxiety vanishes. now i know they are here. we shall go to the village and beat them up.

"comrades, i am not going anywhere," shouts the lieutenant.

"i want to drive to freedom as a decent fighter who has stood in the front line all these years. courage - that's something else. i am not going to risk my life senselessly in some unimportant skirmish. now, right at the end!"

the comrades exchange murmurs.

"we can't hesitate!" i shout out angrily, from a full chest. "the dilemma of this moment is ridiculous. until we have swept the enemy away forever, we are only demi-victors. can a demi-freedom be real freedom? vermin must be destroyed if they stand in our way! all, everything that has sucked our blood! away with the suffocating past, let pure freedom live!"

"let it live!" "hurrah!" "let's go!" the fighters join in.

the lieutenant marches up to the hayhouse, seating himself in the car. "i am staying here. i too have the right to a my grave? shall i fall so that others can feast themselves upon my grave? i've already fought for freedom and now why shouldn't i enjoy it?"

"i shall wait for freedom to come and get me," replies the lieutenant.

WHY DO THESE BLACK WORMS FLY JUST EVERYWHERE I AM MYSELF ONLY ACCIDENTALLY

my childhood was full of stories about the war. past war, whose heavy blow never ceased to suffocate my mother. her stories were no hymn to heroism. she escaped from torture, fled from the wall of hostages, survived the concentration camp – and yet she was always retelling her own disbelief about having deluded death.

the fear from violent, out of hatred and vengeance arising death, was the only fear i could never live with. i wrote in the school paper: "my biggest wish is, there will never be a war". but my mother has always asked me to burn her body after her death. "i can't stand the thought of being devoured by worms", she was explaining her vision of inevitable absurd. i was feeling this absence of reason during the entire life as an unfinished though invincible wall of intolerance and as impenetrable glasses of unconcern. now i don't even know anymore when the absurd adopted a face and began to walk around here. i remember the most persisting was my bullet–proof jacket, when on the street next to mine a helicopter was shut down; persisting was my helmet, when shooting was taking place under my window, persisting dragged me away, when a missile exploded above me; persisting protected me from panic of people i had been spending hours and hours in the shelter with. later on persisting became a filter put in front of a TV screen. persisting is just a rampart against the emotions that try to break through as a mountain torrent into me, to tear me up and drag away into the flood of war. on friday goran with his friends came from osijek. they were showing off video tapes of the destroyed town, they were displaying pictures of dead bodies, they were reciting missives of the attacked ones, they were singing... "to document, not to interpret" he said, being composed and submitted as never before. he is also persisting. he travels incessantly through the enemy–encirclements, taking the war from osijek to zagreb, rijeka, hungary, czechoslovakia, germany – and afterwards he goes back.

to persist.

we were facing each other, two empty mirrors, from which the images were erased by persistence, we were exchanging speechless words and just feeling, how slowly, but in perseverantly increasing number, we get eaten by worms. our encounter was simple, short and completely inexplicable, like death.

November 16th 1991

116

ANDREJ BLATNIK

Translated by Tamara Soban

Andrej Blatnik, born 1963 in Ljubljana, works as an editor. Played bass guitar in a punk band and travelled, in Japan supported by a government grant. Published a novel 'Torches and Tears' (1987) and three books of short stories: 'Bouquets for Adam Fade' (1983), 'Biographies of the Nameless' (1989), 'Skinswaps' (1990). Author of several radio dramas. Translated American literature (Anais Nin's 'Delta of Venus', Sylvia Plath's 'The Bell Jar', Stephen King's 'Pet Sematary' etc.). His short stories have been translated and published in English, German, French, Spanish, Italian, Croatian, Serbian, Polish and Albanian.

BILLIE HOLIDAY

What if, she says, we played that old Billie Holiday record? Would you kiss me then?

You don't have it any more, he says. You haven't got that record any more.

How do you know? she asks. There are some things one never looses.

But not that record, he says. Do you remember how we searched for it last year? That time we went to the cinema and were both very sad afterwards, and we got drunk and looked for that record and it wasn't anywhere, and we just danced, without music. Don't you remember?

Yes, I remember, she says. But we got drunk that time and we didn't look everywhere. The record could have still been here some place, it's just that we didn't find it.

And you found it afterwards? he asks. You?

I do the cleaning in this apartment, in case you've already forgotten, she says quietly. I'm the one who goes rummaging through the closets.

And now you have it? Do you have it? he asks, a trifle impatiently.

It doesn't matter, she says quietly. I don't think it matters.

No? he says. You don't?

You didn't answer my question, she says. You didn't tell me.

What? he says.

Well, she says, if you'd kiss me.

If we had the record?

If I had the record.

What does that mean – if I had?

It's mine, isn't it? You bought it for me, for my birthday. Don't you remember?

He remains silent.

Yes, I remember, he says slowly. Yes, that's right.

It's also written on it, she says. It says: to you, the one and only. And your name is on it. And the date.

Is it? he says.

Yes. Don't you remember?

I remember, he says, quite slowly, not sounding very convinced.

You've forgotten, she says, you've forgotten. To you, the one and only. You forgot everything. And you won't even kiss me any more. Not even if I play that record. Because you think it's too late. Don't you?

What? he says.

Don't be evasive, she says. You know what I'm talking about. That's what you think, isn't it?

He says nothing. When he finally breaks the silence, his voice is hoarse and it breaks against the walls of the room.

Wouldn't it be better, he says, if people solved things like this in some other way? Differently?

In what way? she asks. How differently?

With less...pain. More easily.

And how do you imagine that? she says slowly.

Let's say: write about it to the papers. And then people would respond. Give advice. They would say: it happened to me too, and then...

Dear Abby?

Dear Abby.

And how would this help? Advice? We've had more than enough advice, everybody told us their story, everyone has one. And it was no use.

Even if it was no use, he says. It would be there. It's easier if you know you're not the only one it's happened to.

You mean like you said the other day: that it's necessary to distribute the pain equally? she asks. That everyone gets an equal share of it? And that this way it's easier for everyone?

Yes, he nods seriously. That's it.

Interesting, she says. Interesting.

What, he asks. What's interesting?

She opens her mouth, and he, against his will, notices how this mouth is smaller than the one he remembers. Something is missing, he thinks. No, not missing – it has grown smaller.

The telephone rings.

The phone's ringing, she says.

I can hear it, he says, it's ringing. And now what?

Answer it. Pick it up. It's for you, I'm sure.

What if it isn't? Maybe it's for you.

It's never for me, she says. Nobody ever calls me. It is for you.

He picks up the receiver. Hello? he says. Oh, it's you, he says then. How are you?

While the voice at the other end of the line is answering, he covers the receiver with his palm and whispers: You were right. It really is for me.

It's her, isn't it? she says.

It's her, he nods seriously, and then immediately says into the receiver: oh, yeah? Is that so? Really?

She turns and leaves the room. He keeps glancing at her, while speaking smoothly into the telephone: Mhm. Yes. You don't say!

Music is heard from the adjoining room. He frowns and says into the telephone: what?

She returns, leans against the wall and looks at him. The corners of her mouth curve, and then drop again. And a few more times like that.

He says into the telephone: this? Billie Holiday.

She nods. Yes, Billie Holiday, she says quietly.

He says: old, of course it's old.

She steps close to him and puts her arms around his waist.

He says: I like it.

She leans her head against his belly.

He says: what? No, I'm not alone.

She gives him a strong hug.

He says: she's here. Near me.

She draws his shirt out of his trousers.

He says: what do you mean, how near? Yes, she's in this room. Yes, close enough to touch.

She draws her palm across his skin.

He says, somewhat reluctantly: I don't know. He covers the receiver and mouths a question.

She says, loudly, as if they were alone: what?

He keeps covering the receiver, and whispers: she's asking if you mind my talking to her.

I do mind, she says calmly. And continues to caress his skin.

He removes his hand from the receiver and wipes the sweat from his forehead. She doesn't mind, he says unconvincingly into the telephone.

Did she fall for it? she asks.

He nervously covers the receiver with his hand.

What? he says. No, that's music. Billie Holiday.

She rises, steps close to him and kisses him on the mouth.

He takes hold of her chin and turns her face away, but not with much conviction.

Of course I love you, he says into the receiver.

Tell her you're lying, she says quietly. Tell her.

Really, he says. I do.

You know you love me, she says with determination. Me. Although you don't show it. Although you think you shouldn't show it.

He lets the hand holding the receiver dangle at his hip. How do you know? he says.

Your skin tells me, she says calmly. At night, when we're lying together, in the same bed, your skin tells me: I love you.

How's that? he says. My skin?

Skin talks, she says with conviction. Didn't you know?

No, I didn't, he admits.

There's a lot more you don't know, it seems to me, she says, somehow compassionately.

He looks at her for a while, then drops his eyes and notices the receiver in his hand. What did you say? he says. And waits.

Then he hangs up.

She' no longer there, he says.

That's the way it should be, she says. She hung up. She knew you were lying. Like I know.

No, he objects, I'm not lying.

The skin, she says. Your skin gives you away.

My skin? he says and draws his palm across his cheek. What's all this about skin?

Yeah, what about it? she asks. Why don't you listen to it any more? Why don't you follow it? Why do you want to get out of it?

Listen? Follow? Out? he asks. Hey, listen, what's your game? What are you trying to tell me?

That you don't know how to listen, she says calmly. And that's why you think that all things come to an end. That they pass away and are gone. That they disappear without a trace. While in reality they're still there, only different. If you listened, you'd know.

I don't understand, he says.

You don't understand because you don't listen, she says. Everything lasts. It's true that it sometimes isn't the way it used to be, it's true that it sometimes looks old and out of style. But it lasts. Just a sort of film covers it. And everything is the same as it used to be. The same beautiful things. Just a little...older. And that's why they look strange to you.

Like Billie Holiday? he says. Beautiful, but old. And that's why it crackles.

That's right. Like Billie Holiday.

But we lost it, he says to himself.

And found it again, she says.

You found it, he says. You. I...I'm just listening. From a distance.

Once you said, she says, that everything looked beautiful that way. From a distance. Because you could imagine it your way.

Once, he says, once I had all the answers. I knew everything. What. Why. How.

And know it's over, she says. You don't have any answers any more. But you still have something. Something more.

What? he asks.

Me, she says. You've got me.

I can't, he says. You know it doesn't work that way.

What way? she asks.

You're not enough. I have to eat. I have to sleep, I have to ...

What? she say. What else? Tell me.

What else am I supposed to say? he says.

Her, she says. You haven't mentioned her.

Why does it always end with her? he says, bad–tempered. Why does everything lead to her in the end?

Yes, why? she says thoughtfully. Why, when in reality...

The music stops.

What is it? he starts. Is it the end of the record?

Wait, she says. There's more.

And really, in the next room Billie Holiday starts singing again.

The sky was blue
And high above
The moon was new
And so was love...

That's what you sang to me when we were at the seaside, he grows tender.

No, no, she says.

Yes, he continues. Quite a while ago. When we walked along the beach in the evening, and you told me which star was which. I was absolutely enchanted; I don't know anything about stars.

No, no, she persists.

Yes, nothing. And then we sat down somewhere by the sea. It looked like the middle of nowhere, remember? And we drank all the fruit–brandy we could get into that little flask you gave me when you were selling them at the Christmas fair. And you held my hand a little longer every time I handed you the drink.

That wasn't me, she says with determination.

No? he says incredulously.

No.

That's right, he grows pensive. Her skin was cooler than yours.

Was it?

Yes. Cool and smooth.

And mine isn't?

I know every pore on your skin.

Pore? she says.

Crease and scratch, he says, somewhat impatiently.

And that's why you don't want it any more, she says calmly. Are there many?

I don't know, he says. But I know them all.

They do no harm, she says. It's like Billie Holiday's records. Scratches belong there. Without them it would be something different.

That's just it, he says.

It – what?

It – something different.

So that's what it's all about, she says. You're fed up. And you think it'll take your mind off it, if it's something different. And that you won't notice that it's sometimes the same as it was before. Because you're the same. It's the same, except for the scratches that come after a long time.

No, he says. What are you talking about? That's nonsense.

Nonsense, she nods. As always. The same, I tell you.

The telephone rings again.

Let it ring, she says. It'll stop.

Aren't you interested in who it is? he asks. It might be for you.

I know who it is, she says. It's not for me.

If it isn't for you, he says, then it's for me. And if it's for me, I really don't see why I shouldn't answer it.

Because you don't have time, she says.

I don't have time? What am I doing that is so important that I don't have time?

You're listening to Billie Holiday.

I think I can listen to Billie Holiday and talk on the phone. Both at the same time. I think I can manage that.

No, you can't. Not if you listen to Billie Holiday and kiss me at the same time. Then you can't talk on the phone.

Listen to Billie Holiday and kiss you? Like in the old times?

That's right. Only with more scratches. With the coating. With everything that came along. And so, differently.

But look, the phone won't stop ringing. It just keeps ringing. I can't listen to Billie Holiday with the phone ringing all the time. I can't kiss you if it's ringing, and it's for me, and I know who it is.

Well, then answer and tell her, she says. Tell her what you're doing. And it'll stop ringing. And it'll be easier.

He looks at her. He looks at the telephone. He looks at his hand hovering over the receiver.

127

I should tell her? Really? And if I do tell her – what'll happen then? Will it be any different? Changed in any way?

Tell her. There are things that don't seem to exist unless you say them. Maybe this one isn't that kind... But then, maybe it is. Tell her, and we'll see what happens next.

He picks up the receiver. He looks at her again, and she nods. He also lifts his head and bends it upon his chest in a slow arc. Singing is still heard from the background. The record is crackling slightly.

I can't, he says into the receiver held in his outstretched arm, far away from his mouth. I can't. I'm listening to Billie Holiday. Still. In the same way. But differently. Do you hear? Do you understand?

KYOTO

"Tea-drinking," said Jay, "is a skill that takes years to learn, if not decades."

We looked at each other. We had taken these words rather well, we felt. Nobody had screamed. We were holding our china cups tightly in our palms. Then we heard a polite cough from the back of the room. We turned around, though we need not have.

Of course, it was Sam, who else could it have been.

"Excuse me," he started unctuously, "did you say – years?"

"Years," nodded Jay seriously. "If not decades."

"But," Sam smiled somewhat uncertainly, "I'm staying in Kyoto only for another week or so. No, even less. Actually, five days."

Well, in that case you will never know how to drink tea, we thought.

"In that case the art of drinking tea will probably stay unknown to you forever," Jay said obligingly.

Now he will say: but..., we thought.

"But..." said Sam with disapproval.

But what? we thought. What in the world, 'but'? Everything is clear.

"Yes, I am listening to you," Jay said kindly. "Is anything the matter?"

He will object, saying that he came to Kyoto with the sole purpose of learning how to drink tea.

"I came to Kyoto with the sole purpose of learning how to drink tea," objected Sam.

Jerk! we thought. So you came in vain.

"I can understand your point of view," said Jay. "In this case, I am afraid your decision to come to Kyoto might not have been the right one."

Now he will want him to explain it in detail, we were horrified, now he will begin with: are you saying...

"Are you saying," began Sam, "that my coming here was completely useless? In your brochure it was written that the mystery of tea was accessible to everyone who came to your school. And that's why I came to Kyoto, after all. What I'm saying is: I am here, I had to pay for the trip, I have to pay for my hotel room, I even had to pay for coming to your school, and now..."

So you threw your money away, probably not for the first time, nor the last either! we thought.

Jay smiled. "Some people say," he said, »that the whole point of money is to spend it."

"Yes, yes," Sam refused to be distracted," but the ways are different, you'll have to admit that much, different. I could have given my money to the poor..." He paused dramatically.

"People do that, true," remarked Jay, "and it is probably not the worst of possibilities at our disposal."

"...nor I could have invested it in some company that would then fail..."

Stop, stop, we thought. You are being a nuisance. Go away, this thing is simply not for you. Why should our teacher concern himself with you when you do not want to learn? Let him take interest in us. But he is so patient, he will let you go on nagging him...

"You might have regretted that," inferred Jay sympathetically.

"No more than I regret my coming to Kyoto. You must understand me, I really can't dedicate years and decades to such a simple thing as drinking tea," Sam was resolute.

"A simple thing? Did you say a simple thing?" said Jay with amazement.

"Of course. Let's be realistic: any child can drink tea." "Good Lord! Just the preparation of tea according to the rules of our school takes four hours and requires hundreds of precise and elaborate gestures which take years to learn! And drinking comes only after that!"

"And where does this very special way of drinking get you?" asked Sam.

Now, at last, Jay will scratch his eyes out, we said to ourselves. Otherwise, we will be forced to do it ourselves. After all, now he is wasting our time, our money, our admission fee.

"I am holding a cup of tea in my hands," began Jay. "In its green colour I can see all nature. When I close my eyes, I discover green hills and pure water in my heart. When in silence, alone with myself, I sit and drink tea, I feel how it is all becoming a part of me. And when I share this cup of tea with others, they also become one, with me and with nature –"

Don't interrupt him, we thought, just don't interrupt –

"This," interrupted Sam, "is utter mumbo jumbo. And a little pathetic at that. Cheap Oriental mystique, actually quasi–mystique."

Jay observed him silently for a long time, and we started glancing towards the door. Yes, it was time to leave, we thought. And not only for Sam. After all, we did get something for our money – a few nice words and a cup of tea, if that thickish bitter liquid is to be called that. We did as we had been told: you put your cup into your right palm, turn it twice clockwise, finish the tea in three swallows, again turn the cup twice in the opposite direction... and that's that, as far as the first lesson is concerned.

"I am not an Oriental, sir," finally said Jay. "I am an American, like you."

That is right, we thought. He is American. We said to ourselves: this could be a turnabout. We waited to see what would happen next. Anything was possible now, and especially sentences like: then you of all people should know that the ratio between the capital invested and value created should be in your favor! Or perhaps: this doesn't absolve you in the critical eye of history! Or even: traitor! you betrayed your people!

"If you're American," said Sam smugly, pleased with himself, as if he had finally achieved what he had been wanting to all along, "you won't reject my proposal."

For the first time now, Jay was slightly perplexed. "What do you propose?" he asked cautiously.

"A small bet. If you win, I'll immediately write out a cheque for one hundred thousand dollars to your school. I'll take out my cheque–book right away."

We all drew in our breath. So did Jay. One hundred thousand! Like hell! Only last night he let us pay for his beer!

"Money does not mean much to us teachers of tea," Jay replied uncertainly.

"Oh, well, in that case forget about my proposal," Sam shrugged ingenuously, and the lurking way he was observing Jay did not escape our notice.

"And what if you should win the bet?" the question almost eluded Jay's control.

"Well, in that case you'll come with me, back to America."

"I do not want to go to America," Jay was surprised. "I can not live without tea any more."

"You won't be without tea in America," said Sam. "I'll open a school of tea. Americans won't have to go to Kyoto any more to get the proper education, and the whole business will be cheaper in America, due to travel expenses, among other things."

"But we already have schools of tea in America," said Jay cautiously. "One in New York, one in Seattle and one in Honolulu."

So, we thought, Sam could not make much profit on this thing. Of course he could not be competitive with his total lack of understanding of the essence of tea. He will really go back empty-handed from his trip, poor guy.

"That's good," said Sam soberly. "It shows that it can also work in America. The only thing left for me to do is establish our school better than your branch schools. And this shouldn't be too complicated. We'll promote our firm as a genuine American school of tea-drinking and not as a branch of a Japanese firm."

We could not help rolling our eyes at the things he said. Who for heaven's sake drinks tea in America, let alone teaches others how to do it? It was clear to everyone, except obviously to Sam, that you can not sell the art of tea-drinking unless you play upon eastern exotica.

Jay refused to be drawn. He said warily: "If I am not mistaken, you mentioned a sort of bet."

"Yes, a bet," said Sam. "are you interested?"

It's obvious, we thought, it's too obvious.

"Well, in a way," Jay said, apparently without much interest.

It was clear. He was interested. He was very interested.

"The thing is very simple," said Sam. "You claimed before that thanks to the tea skills you had become one with nature. It's just a matter of proving this."

We waited. Sam waited. Jay waited.

"The thing is," continued Sam, "last night, for instance, I was going back to my hotel late at night. I was walking in a deserted district, I could see the eyes of wild animals glittering in the dark, I could hear terrifying snarls..."

We listened in amazement. What is he talking about? We were all staying together, in the Grand Hotel, two hundred meters from the railroad station, and the highway ran beside it. What eyes of wild animals, what snarling? Japan is so densely populated you can walk for days on end without finding a spot you could not see a neon sign from. And he says: a deserted district.

Jay listened silently. Perhaps he never goes out of this little bamboo room, we thought, and he does not know what the world is like outside. But it would have been enough for him to look at the city map to see there were no thickets like the one Sam was describing anywhere, let alone one with a hotel for Americans in it.

"... and so it occurred to me that, for thousands of years, people have actually been inventing all sorts of implements to subjugate nature somehow, while at the same time they've failed to understand it completely, they don't see its quintessence, they only see its deceptive forms of appearance..."

We looked at Jay; he was nodding thoughtfully. A simple-minded person would have said that he had taken the bait.

"... and therefore they'll never know how to become one with it. They'll always remain strangers in the world, doomed to endless struggle without hope of success..."

We exchanged meaningful glances. What philosophy! It made us feel as if we were sitting at home in front of the TV and watching commercials.

"...and the only possibility they have of not being defeated in this struggle is to become reconciled with the fact that they had actually lost it at the time when they separated from nature, when man became a super-species. But it's precisely because they are a super-species that they can not become reconciled with it."

Undoubtedly Jay chewed well on the bait. To him Sam's words probably exuded the aroma of koans, of *Mumonkan*, and he was attracted to such fragrances. He became impatient. He said: "Yes, yes, certainly... And what would the bet be?"

Now, we knew, the letdown must follow. It must become apparent that this bet is actually nothing special...

"Actually, it's nothing special," said Sam coaxingly. "It's simply that…"

If he said 'simply', this is going to be a long story, we thought wearily.

"Last night, for instance, our hotel shook. Nothing unusual, nothing unexpected. An earthquake. A very frequent thing in these parts. Tectonic agitations. In short, an everyday occurrence. Well, you know the way it is. In our hotel, we Americans are mixed with the Japanese. And not just us. What I'm trying to say is that the hotel has a racially mixed clientele. And when yesterday's earthquake happened, it became apparent that what was at issue here was more than just the colour of the skin. All the whites came rushing to the hotel lobby, everyone grabbing what they could, we were all in pajamas, thrown out of our sleep…"

This time only a few of us exchanged glances, perhaps the ones who had slept soundly all night and, to use a phrase, had not even dreamt of it.

"… but only us, the whites, and not a single Asian – or what should I call them. And this really makes one think that there might be, after all, something in this tea–link with nature. Maybe people who drink tea really are somehow one with nature…"

Well, maybe, we thought, the Japanese have simply gotten so accustomed to such little earthquakes that they simply can not be bothered.

"Not all the Orientals drink tea," Jay ventured.

"But still," Sam persisted, "all the same!"

All the same – what? we wondered. Maybe even Sam could not have answered that.

"And the bet?" asked Jay. It was evident – his calm was crumbling; at a sum that continued to dance in front of everyone's eyes his calm was disappearing like shaving foam under a razor. The bet, of course, the bet. Now things can not go on without the bet.

135

"Is it a bet then?" said Sam, now on the lookout with his whole being. "Shall we bet?"

The atmosphere grew electric. Jay undoubtedly felt there was something behind this offer. He must have felt it. It was in the air. We could have touched it – if we had dared to reach out. Jay probed each one of us with his eyes, as if he were trying to find in us, who were supposed to know Sam better than he did, the answer to the question: what lies behind all this? But our eyes were cast downward, although we could have looked him straight in the eye; we did not know what lay behind.

"Well, perhaps I might bet," admitted Jay, increasingly prudently, "but you should tell me first what the bet actually consists of."

"It's simple," hastened Sam, and we were horrified at this word, "if I'm not mistaken you claim that you become one with nature when drinking tea..." He paused significantly.

"Yes," confirmed Jay.

"With all living creatures..." Another pause.

"Yes," repeated Jay.

"So that you form a harmonious whole with all living beings..."

"Yes."

"...and that nothing natural is alien to you, that nothing living disgusts you..."

"Yes."

"Well, in that case," concluded Sam triumphantly, "eat this."

He bent to the ground and reached for something. We all turned to look at him, we all looked down his extended arm, our eyes boring into his closed fist. No, we were not quick enough, we were not as quick as he was. We did not see anything.

Jay dashed towards him. "What? What?" he asked nervously. He no longer tried to hide that he was completely perplexed; perhaps he was aware that he was unable to conceal it. We stepped closer, too; we formed a circle around Jay and Sam. We stretched our necks in curiosity. Sam was clutching his find, which was to decide about one hundred thousand dollars, in his fist. The absurdity of the situation quickened our heart beat. We were waiting for Jay to tell him to show what he had.

"Show me what you have," said Jay.

Sam slowly opened his fist.

On his palm crouched a five centimeter long and proportionately fat caterpillar. Automatically we first wondered how he had managed to find such a loathsome thing in the middle of immaculate Japan, and we were at first on the point of accusing him of having brought it with him. Then we had a good look at the animal. It was covered with thick shaggy hair, which made it look all the more repulsive. Besides that, it started to tremble all along its length, as if it felt the weight of our looks upon it. Watching that quivering nasty thing made one's eyes smart.

"Eat this," repeated Sam.

Jay gaped at him, and a sickly bluish pallor gradually covered his face; we could see it descending from his straight cut hair down to his neck. Of course, it is not an easy task, we thought, but for one hundred thousand dollars, one would swallow hard even after a morsel like this. Besides, the Japanese – as we had learned in the hotel dining–room – were used to taking into their mouths a lot of things we could not even bear to look at. It is true that Jay is American, we said to ourselves, but in Japan he probably does not have ham and eggs for breakfast everyday, as we do, who are only visiting here.

"This?" he asked slowly, very slowly, as if he wanted to give Sam ample time to change his mind. "You can't be serious. This?"

"This," replied Sam.

Jay looked around him uncertainly. We followed his look and saw whatžhe did, what he saw day in and day out, while we had not noticed before, and – immersed in musings about tea skills – might otherwise never have noticed: the cracks in the walls of the tea school, the rush mats frayed at the edges, the stains on the ceiling indicating that the water–resistant paint was giving way. Perhaps, if one drinks enough tea, one does not notice water dripping on one's head, we thought mischievously.

"Will you take the bet?" asked Sam. We waited. We waited for quite a while. And then, suddenly, Jay turned around and reached into Sam's open hand. In all probability he never closed his mouth from the moment he saw what Sam had picked up from the floor, and now he raised his hand to his mouth, leaving behind Sam's palm empty. We realized: he was trying to be faster than his second thoughts, faster than disgust. And he succeeded: his hand did not hesitate before his mouth, he withdrew it in the same motion, and swallowed loudly. We saw his Adam's apple bob, and the veins in his neck stand out. Then his eyes bulged and we saw him shudder, close his eyes and go weak at the knees. We looked at Sam. Now he was pale, paler than Jay had been before. Obviously he had not expected such an outcome, after all, and, regarding the way he let others pay for his drinks, he probably did not enjoy squandering money very much.

It serves you right, we thought spitefully. Now take out your cheque–book, you arrogant fool. And write the figure, right to the last zero. We are all witnesses. If only you had to sell every single thing you possess to pay off the debt!

At that moment a frightening groan escaped Jay's lips. He turned on his heels and fell to his knees. During the fall, the contents of his stomach burst out of his mouth, and he left a trail of half–digested food on the wall, oozing slowly towards the floor. Eventually, his body stopped shivering, and only mucus came from his mouth. He wiped his mouth on the sleeve of his blue coat, in the armpit of which we thought we could see sewn–on patches for a moment. The earned money will come in handy for his tea school, we thought. And he can now be considered a sort of hero. He is a hero, too. Which one of us would have done this – for someone else's sake?

"Start writing the cheque," croaked Jay in a glassy voice. He wanted to lean his hand on the wall, but he placed it exactly on the trail he had left during his fall and at the touch of something wet he looked up, and the sight of what was directly in front of him made him jerk his hand back, so that his body swayed dangerously and it seemed that he would fall into the middle of his own vomit. But he caught himself. He regained his balance.

We looked at Sam. He looked at us. He could see in our faces the final affirmation of what he already knew: that there was no way out for him. Then he looked at Jay. He gazed at him for a long time, as if spellbound by the painful sight. And suddenly something caught his attention, something wriggling on the floor, in the vomit. He bent down to see better, and when he pulled himself erect again, his face shone with triumph.

"I'm afraid you haven't won the bet after all," he said. "the pest is still here."

We drew near, and true enough, there in the filth squirmed the caterpillar. It did not appear to have been affected in any way by those few seconds spent in Jay's insides.

Jay – with great effort – also took a look, and as soon as he was convinced of the truth of the matter, he closed his eyes in despair.

"Actually, you lost the bet," continued Sam. "You have by no means become one with this caterpillar, no, we couldn't say that you have become one with it at all. Or" he turned to us, "would someone wish to claim that, despite everything?"

Against our will, we shook our heads. One thing was clear: none of us would pay for his beer any more. Not any more.

"That part about becoming one with nature was meant in a more spiritual sense," said Jay weakly. "To become one also physically, it should become part of me. And for that I would have to murder it."

"That's right," said Sam. "You'd have to murder it, if that's what you call it."

"Murder," said Jay, "murder..."

"Don't speak now as if you had some great qualms about it," retorted Sam. "You had no qualms before. You were blinded by the money and didn't think it was murder at all."

Jay blushed scarlet, now in the opposite direction, from his neck up to the crown of his head. Slowly and carefully he was drawing himself erect.

"Yes," he said tiredly. "Yes. I was blinded by the money. Perhaps it really is time for me to return to America. Perhaps I do not belong here, in Japan. Perhaps I never have belonged here."

"What is Japan nowadays but a poor quality instant copy of America?" asked Sam, aloof. "What else are all these McDonald's, all these slot-machine halls, all these copied metropolitan streets, all this neon and metal?"

"This," said Jay, "is Japan without tea. Japan, which does not know how to drink tea any more. They still drink it, but they do not know how to drink it any more." He went towards the door. "I am going to pack my luggage. When are we leaving?"

"Let me tell you something," said Sam. "That tea almost made me throw up."

We could kill him, it occurred to us. Tonight we could fill him up with drink – if we paid for the drinks, he would surely get blind drunk – and when he fell asleep, we could break into his room and we could...

Jay waved us off with his hand. "Go," he said. "Go. I'll find you at the Grand Hotel. And then we'll go home. Home." Absent-mindedly he started to chuckle.

Really, we could kill him, we thought as we were going up the steps to board the bus, while we were riding along the wide avenues of Kyoto, when our slant-eyed guide first asked us how our tea school had been. Lamely, we muttered it had been wonderful, and then she went on to explain all about this or that temple or this or that imperial palace. We could kill him, we thought towards the evening, as the outlines of *Kinkaku-ji*, the Golden Pavilion, were sinking behind us in the twilight, and we were still thinking about it the next day, as we were hauling our luggage to the *shinkansen*, and speeding at 220 kilometers per hour towards Tokyo, towards the Narita airport, towards home, leaving Kyoto and the tea school behind us at an incredible speed. We could kill him, but we will not, because civilized people do not do that out of outrage and disgust, but for more substantial reasons. No, together with him and Jay we will return to our country, live there as we had before, we will try to remember our visit to Japan just by the chemical layers on our slides, and at night we will dream about the green dollar bills, they will appear in front of our eyes, one by one, all the hundred thousand of them, and at that sight there will be a pleasant tinge down our throats, as if we had managed to swallow that caterpillar and keep it down, and, whenever we have a chance, we will talk about how Western man has lost his true bond with nature, and we will travel only to the places where our neighbours have already been and returned without any shocks, and our children will decide to get away from our philistine way of life, from our narrow-minded bourgeois views, and perhaps, on their flight, they will enroll in the very school of tea that Sam is going to open, and it will be Jay who will teach them about tea, the one and the same Jay we saw fall to his knees and throw up because he was disgusted to become one with a part of nature.

ISAAC

For days on end they were being driven in sealed boxcars, where night had no end. At first they tried to guess what was waiting for them at the end of the journey, later they just prayed. Nobody complained about hunger and thirst any longer, they had all come to terms with that, only Isaac crouched in a corner and persistently worked away at the hardwood floor with his fingernails. The hours went by and he felt his fingers turning into raw, shapeless lumps. When he looked around at his fellow passengers, he saw that their faces were transfigured, already contemplating the next world. He knew that in their present state they could no longer understand his plan. He had to do it on his own. When he was on the point of thinking that his strength had run out and that he would join them in prayer, light seeped through a crack in the floor.

Then the hole widened quickly. Soon it was big enough for him to see through to the cross–ties rushing by. Then it was so wide that he knew they could squeeze themselves through it, after all the starving they had gone through in the wooden cage. He nudged the man sitting next to him. "Let's go," he said. "We can go." The man looked at him, bewildered, and when Isaac saw his eyes in the daylight coming through the scratched-out floor, he felt almost sorry for disturbing him. "Pray," the man whispered kindly, "Pray." He stretched his arm as if to put it around Isaac's shoulders. Isaac drew away from him and the man's arm dropped

142

limp by his side. "I'm going," Isaac said out loud. "Here's a way out". "Pray," the quiet murmur was all around him, although nobody had lifted their head. "Pray."

They've gone crazy with the suffering, he thought. Prayer won't save them. They're going to die. Die. Then it occurred to him that they might not be praying for salvation after all, that they might be just trying to prepare themselves for the inescapable, but there was not much difference between the two explanations to him. He squeezed himself through the opening. He touched the ground feet first and the cross-ties struck his heels; the dull thumps felt good, they made him aware that he was not just running away in a dream. Then he let go. It did not hurt him at all, he only felt the blood ooze from the scratches. He lay on his back, stretched completely flat, and watched the under-frames and wheels race by. The train was a long one and many a car had passed over him when he suddenly realized in horror that it was slowing down. It was true; the train was coming to a stop. Then there were no cars left and he was blinded by daylight. Behind him, he heard the screeching of the brakes. When he regained his eyesight the first and only thing he saw was a highly polished army boot. He looked up. The officer was unbuckling his holster. "We've arrived. Were you leaving us?" he inquired, smiling. Isaac tried to jump up, to run away, but all his strength had deserted him. His limbs filled with air, and then suddenly his memory was flooded by his entire life, by the endless journey, and his hands started to hurt terribly. "Animal," he breathed hard, "animal." For a moment he wondered what he had meant by that – they had been driven like animals, he would die like an animal, and, actually, he had also lived like an animal, without respect for the faith of his forefathers–but he realized that this kind of thinking was now irrelevant and trivial. The officer bent towards him; Isaac could see the well-oiled gun glitter in the sunlight. "I may be an animal," he said, "but this animal is philosophical. If you can't change the fate of the majority, you have to share it with them." He aimed his gun at Isaac's head and Isaac wondered: will I feel anything at all? Then, in the split second he had remaining, he realized that beyond the barrel of the gun there was awaiting *Shekinah*.

HIS MOTHER'S VOICE

I n the cinema the kid was watching a horror film. People were screaming in terror. On the screen, an invisible killer was killing off, one by one, the members of a family living in a lonely spot – a house on the outskirts of town. They had not done anything, or if they had, it was not clear what it was; he was killing them, as it were, because it was their fate. All the murders happened in more or less the same way; each time a member of the family would unsuspectingly enter a room where the killer was waiting in ambush for them, and he would slaughter them. Each time the audience would groan: how could they be so stupid! They should have known there was a killer in the house, and yet they were not at all careful. Not even the soft, harmonious whisper that was heard whenever the killer was close meant anything to them, although it was loaded with significance.

The most horrible scene of all was where the killer called to the little son of the family, who had suspected that something was wrong and was determined to act with utmost caution. He did it by imitating his mother's voice. The little boy naively believed that it really was his mother calling him, while in reality she was lying in a pool of blood on the floor, at the killer's feet. Somebody sitting next to the kid whispered: "Be careful, watch out, it's not your mommy, it's not your mommy." At the peak of suspense a woman cried out: "Run!" The little boy did not hear her and did not run away. He went straight to the killer. Everything was clear.

The kid drew in his lips and stared at the screen. He kept repeating to himself that it was just a movie. The killer cut the child to pieces before the little boy could realize that he had made a wrong move, that it had not been his mother. The people felt somehow relieved that it was all over. They had known all along that the little boy would not make it, he was too gullible, it could not have ended any differently, they told themselves. The kid thought: how could he have been so careless and not have recognized the voice? If he had recognized it, he might have been able to defend himself. If only he hadn't let himself be drawn to that room!

Soon afterwards the killer was identified and the film was over. The lights went on in the cinema. People were getting up from their seats and straightening their clothes. Each one somewhat hesitated at the exit, as if unwilling to go out, and then went off into the darkness. The kid was among the last to leave. It was the first time his mother had let him go to the late show, and he was scared. He had a long way to go home, as they lived on the outskirts of town, on a lonely spot, and because of the energy saving cuts the electricity was turned off at ten, so the streets were not lit. In every bush the kid thought he could see the killer, and while walking he listened intently to every sound, as he could not see anything. Once he suddenly heard something behind him that strongly resembled the whisper that betrayed the killer's presence, but when he turned around it was only a rat running from one sewer to another.

After a few terror–filled minutes he came home. At first he was almost relieved, thinking that he was safe now and he could tell his mother about how he had been so afraid; the fear would then disappear and they would laugh at it together, as they had many times before. But the house was dark, no lights anywhere. Something seemed wrong. Cautiously, he opened the door. He entered the hall. He waited. He did not know what to do. The house was quiet, almost too quiet. Something's wrong, thought the kid. Something was in there. Something... What if something happened to mommy? They lived in a lonely part of town, anything was possible. If only he had something that would help if... He groped behind the door. He felt something cold under his fingers. He recognized the thing, it was the axe. Yesterday they were chopping wood for the winter with mommy. Mommy praised how strong he had become, since he could split a log in two by himself.

When he took hold of the axe he overturned something and it made a muffled noise. He heard his heartbeat pounding in his ears. He held his breath and waited. The thing inside, in the house, also waited. Then he heard it call out: "Is that you? Kid, is that you?" His first impulse was to drop the axe and enter, then he stopped. It occurred to him that it might not be his mother's voice, although it was similar to it. Very similar. He grasped the handle of the axe firmly. He held it with both hands. Caution. He had to be cautious. Not risk anything. "Kid?" Now the voice seemed even stranger. This was supposed to be his mommy? You're not going to get me, he thought. You're not going to get me.

"Kid, come on in." I'm not going, thought the kid. And I'm not going to run away either. I'll get revenge. You in there, what did you do to her? It's true she let them put me in a special school, so that my schoolmates from the old school don't like me any more, but all the same, she was my mommy, and tonight she let me go to the late show, although it wasn't a children's film. I'll get revenge. "Kid?" He was perplexed. He did not know what to do. The voice was very similar to his mother's. More than the one in the film. How childish that boy in the film was, he thought. No wonder he caught it. He wasn't cautious enough. "Kid? Answer me!" Now the voice was closer. He realized it was coming in the hall. He gathered his strength and lifted the axe above his head. "Are you here? What's the matter?"

By now his eyes had adjusted to the dark. He squeezed himself into the corner behind the door and waited. He imagined his mommy lying on the floor in a pool of blood, and tears came to his eyes. The whisper that betrayed the killer droned in his ears. Here it goes, he thought. The killer's outline was already visible at the door. The kid whimpered in fear and the figure on the doorstep slowly turned towards him. Through the tears and the dark he could see that the killer did not only copy her voice, but also his mother's appearance. The resemblance was amazing. For a moment he faltered. At that moment the killer in the disguise of his mother caught sight of the axe in his hands, and in spite of the dark, the kid could see how it made the killer's eyes widen and the whites stand out. The axe in his uplifted hands trembled and his doubt reached its peak. Then the killer in the guise of his mother screamed in a dreadful way. The scream was like nothing the kid had ever heard before, least of all the warm, kind voice of his mommy. He felt relieved. Now he knew.

THE DAY TITO DIED

It was a Sunday, quite warm, in the afternoon we had been playing frisbees in the street. Then I went in and sat down in front of the tele, and as soon as I heard the music they were playing I knew. I was alone at home, waiting for my mother and father to come home, and in my uneasiness I went to the kitchen and cut myself a slice of bread, I chewed it slowly, the primeval monotonous rhythm of my jaws somehow pacified me. When my mother and father arrived I was just munching the last bite. We sat down at the table and didn't talk, at about ten o'clock in the evening the telephone rang, they were calling me to come to school, and I didn't know what would happen next, my mother and father didn't know either, I put on clean pants and my best shoes and went to school. Some of my teachers and fellow students were there, at first they looked at me strangely, then they said they'd called me because they thought it might be necessary to prepare a commemoration and I was good at those things, but now they'd changed their minds, there would be no commemoration and I could go home. I went home, there was no one in the streets, and at home I got together a few books of partisan and revolutionary poetry in case they still wanted a commemoration the following day, then I lay down on my bed and stared at the ceiling. Only about a year later I learned that right after I'd left home my mother called the school and told them I was ill and they were to leave me alone whatever it was they were doing. That's why they invented the commemoration, sent me home and did whatever it was they were doing without me; what it was I still don't know to this day.